CUNNING

A

NOVEL

by

Susan Peery

Published in the United States by Touchtone Press.

Cover design by Anita Marron.

Cover Photo by William S. Levack

ISBN: 978-0-578-99768-1

Library of Congress Control Number: 2021919564

CUNNING

DEDICATION

For Bobby…The love of my life.
Thank you for your unwavering support
And a special thank you
to my female friends who helped me through a very
tough time..

CONTENTS

PROLOGUE

My eyes flash open. Out of the stillness, I hear a recognizable sound, the front door opening. My heart races. Matt? No, not possible.

I lie motionless and stare at the comforter covering my face, as if some answer to the mess that is my life is going to magically appear. A tear rolls down my cheek and hits the pillow with a dull plop.

I loved him deeply for eight years.

The day I fell in love with him I knew my life would change forever. I just had no idea how true that was going to be or how tragic it would turn out.

Now, sleep has become my only asylum and even that is being disrupted. Not yet ready to be thrust back into reality, a quiet rage grows inside me.

I wait for the house alarm to shriek.

Nothing.

I had probably forgotten to activate it. Over the last few days, I had neglected to do so many things, eat, shower, go to work.

A muffled voice.

Someone is in the house.

Take what you want. Take all of it. I don't care.

I pull back the edge of the comforter to see if the bedroom door is open or closed. An empty vodka bottle tumbles off the bed and hits the floor with a loud thud.

Footsteps approach from the other side of the closed door.

Does the intruder think the house is empty or is he here to kill me, like he had done to the others?

If it is the latter, at least I'll be released from this dark

1

unending nightmare.

PART ONE

THE MOMENT

3

CHAPTER 1

TWO MONTHS EARLIER

The buzzing of the alarm clock jarred me from a peaceful sleep. I jabbed at the off button so as not to awaken the man next to me. *Too late.* A hand snaked around my waist, and I leaned back into his hard, sculpted chest. "Matt is that you?" My husband playfully slapped my bottom and pulled me closer. Some mornings, in those moments between sleep and wakefulness, I actually have to run my hand over the comforter to see if Matt is in bed next to me or if I had dreamt it. That is the downside to being married to an airline pilot, who is absent three to four nights a week.

Matt nuzzled his face against my ear and in a seductive tone asked. "Have time for a quickie?" In an attempt to sway my decision, his hand found its way to my breast, where it gently caressed a nipple.

I moaned, rolled onto my back, and stared into his sexy denim-blue eyes. "It's four-thirty in the morning. I have to shower and …."

His hand explored the shape of my body, and he kissed the edge of my mouth. "Jenn, I'm leaving on a three day trip. You really want to send me away like this?"

His hardness pressed against my thigh, but I knew the question was an idle threat.

Matt would never cheat. We spoke about infidelity before we were married. Long before we met, he had his heart broken by a woman who was sneaking around with a co-worker. Having experienced that betrayal, Matt swore he could never do that to any woman he loved, and I believed him. Matt is safe and loving.

CUNNING

Sure, I've seen the way some women look at him, but luckily, the majority of the flight attendants on the Boeing 717-200 are either gay men or women approaching retirement, nothing a thirty-five-year-old heterosexual captain would sacrifice a happy marriage over.

My thoughts shifted to the new home we were having built in Newnan, Georgia, a small town just south of the Atlanta airport, and Matt's hub.

I whispered in his ear. "I want more mornings like this, so do you think you should stay in Atlanta a few days longer to see how the builder is doing with the changes we requested."

His breath was hot against my neck. "What about our trip to the Bahamas?"

"I was looking forward to a mini-vacation also, but I think we need to stay on top of this, especially if we want construction to be completed by the end of the month." I pulled him on top of me and ran my fingers through his sandy-brown hair. "If it means you'll be home most nights once we move to Atlanta, then I can forgo a visit to the Bahamas."

He slid his fingers between my legs. His touch was electric. When I could no longer take any more, I wrapped my legs around him and we found a perfect rhythm until we reached a crescendo of excitement and pleasure.

When our love-making was over, Matt kissed me, and rolled over to his side of the bed.

I glanced at the clock. Soon it would be dawn. The sex was fun, but it was now time to get serious; mentally prepare for what I had to do.

I crawled out of bed and took a quick shower. Minutes later, I returned to the bedroom to get dressed. Matt had fallen back to sleep.

I watched him for a long moment, then reached into the nightstand drawer and pulled out a Sig Sauer 9mm semi-automatic pistol.

***

I jumped in my car and got on the Sawgrass Expressway heading south to Miami. The drive would have normally taken an hour, but at this early hour, without traffic, I arrived at the darkened bank building in thirty minutes.

A side street led to a back parking lot where I saw the others, members of my squad, the High Intensity Drug Trafficking Area (HIDTA) task force.

It was 5:30, and the morning we had all been waiting for, the arrest of Eduardo Londono, the head of one of the most notorious Miami drug cartels since Griselda Blanco.

Dressed in full raid gear, DEA Agent Paige Higgins walked up to my vehicle in the designated staging area. Paige, a thirty-four-year-old, with shoulder-length ash-blonde hair, and such a lean body you'd never guess that she'd given birth to two children, had an ominous expression on her face.

I braced myself for bad news. "What's going on?"

"Miguel Londono is dead."

Three years earlier the United States Attorney's Office assigned the HIDTA task force the job of dismantling the Londono cartel to prevent another 1980s cocaine cowboy era, which resulted in 621 homicides in one year alone, and required the Dade County Medical Examiner to borrow special refrigerated trucks from Burger King to store the surplus of dead bodies.

Miguel, the younger brother of Eduardo Londono, was a low-level member of the cartel that had been scooped up in the first wave of arrests we made six months earlier. Miguel was not as smart, or as ruthless as his brother. Miguel was weak and foolish. That's how I, a Special Agent with IRS Criminal Investigation, was able to nail him for tax evasion.

My stomach clenched. "How? When?" I asked, not out of concern for the man, but because of the fall-out that would most likely result from his death.

"Heart attack, brain aneurysm, maybe poison. They won't know until the coroner has a look."

I pulled my Kevlar vest over my head. "He was in his fifties, seems too young for a heart attack, and I can't believe any inmate would be stupid enough to harm him, so the smart money is on aneurysm."

Paige motioned for me to follow her over to where the group of law enforcement officers had congregated. "Listen up," she said. "Our Assistant United States Attorney (AUSA) just got a call from the warden at Coleman. Miguel Londono was found dead in his cell at the last bed check, so that means that Eduardo has also been notified." Paige glanced over at me. "Keep your guard up. Eduardo may hold us responsible for his brother's death."

Paige was not only my co-worker, but a dear friend. We frequently partner up, and today was no exception. I jumped into the passenger seat of her car. *Miguel dead.* The words looped through my mind as Paige led the caravan of vehicles to the drug lord's residence. I knew exactly who Eduardo Londono would blame for his brother's death. I was looking at her in the mirrored visor, while tying my long blonde hair back into a pony tail.

CHAPTER 2

With guns drawn, ten agents and a half a dozen local police ran up to the front door of the lavish Coconut Grove home surrounded by palm trees.

Alcohol Tobacco Firearms Agent Neal Phillips, frequently referred to as a Jake Gyllenhaal look-a-like, pounded on the front door and shouted. "Federal agents with a warrant. Open the door or we'll break it down."

Phillips stepped aside and two big burly police officers quickly moved into position, and slammed a huge metal battering ram into the door. The door flew open with only a few pieces of the frame still attached to the wall.

Flowing through the opening like a fierce tidal wave, agents moved rapidly and methodically through the house. ICE Agent Ryan Dees and I peeled off to the right of the living room where I saw a figure run down a hall. In pursuit of the man, I called out to the other agents. "Male subject running toward the back of the house."

The man was trim and fast, definitely not Londono. He ran into a bedroom, and was trying to escape out a sliding door when I tackled him to the floor. A fighter, the man elbowed me in the ribs and crawled to the bed. He was reaching for something in between the box spring and mattress when Dees, a strong muscular agent in his late twenties, along with a powerfully built Miami police officer, pulled the individual's hands behind his back and cuffed him.

With his gloved hand, the police officer retrieved a nine-millimeter Smith and Wesson from under the mattress. After he removed the magazine and cleared the chamber, he slipped the weapon into a clear plastic bag to be placed into evidence.

Paige entered the room and offered her hand to help me up from the floor. A pained grin crossed her face as she collected the pieces of my broken cell phone. "Are you alright?"

I brushed my wispy bangs from my eyes, and stashed what was left of my phone into a pants pocket. "Yeah, I'm fine."

"What's your name?" Dees asked the young Hispanic man, who ignored his question.

A nearby officer pressed the man's thumb against a small portable fingerprint scanner, and read from the screen. "This is Londono's nephew, Enrique. This is Miguel's boy, and he has a prior for possession of illegal firearms."

Dees smirked. "The apple didn't fall far from that tree."

Dees and the police officer walked Enrique out of the house. I followed and watched them place the young man in the back of an unmarked government vehicle.

The sun was rising and neighbors had gathered to watch law enforcement move in and out of the Londono residence.

A minute later, Paige and Neal Phillips exited the house with the overweight sixty-year-old Londono in handcuffs. They placed him in the back seat of Paige's car. After all, it was her drug case and my money laundering investigation that led to his arrest. So, it was only right that we had the pleasure of delivering him to the U.S. Marshals Service.

"Have you heard from Steve?" I asked Dees as I slid into the back seat beside Londono. ICE Agent Steve Rourk, my co-worker and friend, was executing a search warrant on a house that on paper was in Enrique's girlfriend's name.

Dees made direct eye contact with Londono. "Yep, they seized five kilos of cocaine at that location and the other team seized cash at that Cuban restaurant that is in the sister-in-law's name."

Londono stared straight ahead, expressionless.

I grinned at him. "I'll bet those women are going to flip on you and Enrique before lunch. That means your restaurant and the stash house now belong to the United States government. And at the rate things are going, we'll have your entire family in jail by the end of the year."

Dees tapped on the roof of the car. "We'll be right behind you."

No sooner did we hit South Dixie Highway, then Londono fixed his soulless eyes on me. "I know you. You're the one who put my brother behind bars."

The controlled hatred in his voice should have been unnerving. But, it was no match for the anger I felt and the profanity that wanted to spill from my lips.

Days earlier, Londono had my source, Rafael Morales, killed. As if that wasn't bad enough, during the assassin's getaway, he shot and killed two innocent bystanders.

Londono stared at me, waiting for a response.

I swallowed my rage. "He did that to himself. You should have schooled him better in accounting for illegal income."

It made me sick to be seated next to Londono, breathing the same air. I couldn't stop thinking about Rafael's seven-year-old son, who I had met months earlier. "I'm going to be a chef like my daddy," he told me. The last time I saw the little boy he had asked me to keep his daddy safe, an undertaking I did not fulfill.

Londono smirked and a defiant look crossed his sun-weathered face. "You think this is over, but it's not."

I held his gaze for a long minute, then scoffed. "What? You have some get out of jail free card that I don't know about?"

His menacing dark eyes, void of any emotion, sent chills down my spine, but I forged on. "And yes, I do think it is definitely over for you. I brought Rafael Morales before the grand jury weeks ago." As I spoke, I watched the wheels turn in Londono's brain. "Yep, that means that his death locked in his testimony about your money laundering operation. Now, all I have to do is follow the money trail he told me about."

I paused and smiled for effect. "I'm referring to how he created receipts for dinners that were never served to patrons and deposited your illicit cash into the bank matching those fraudulent receipts. Oh, then there's that little trick he played with overstating vendor invoices and again paying with drug money."

Paige's phone rang. She didn't answer. She was laser-focused on the backseat conversation.

The amused expression on Londono's face caused my blood to boil and I did what no person should ever do, prod the Devil. "Just like your brother, your financial house of cards is toppling down because of me. Death came quickly for Rafael, but that's too good for you. I want you in prison so I can watch your mind and body deteriorate in a shit-hole you'll be calling home for the next twenty years."

In the rearview mirror, I saw deep lines form between Paige's eyebrows.

Londono smiled and looked out the window.

We rode in silence until Paige's phone rang again. This time she answered. It sounded like she was talking to Robert Mullaney, the Assistant United States Attorney assigned to the task force. "Our search of the house turned up three weapons and $25,000 in cash. We'll stop by your office after we get Londono processed."

"I want to call my lawyer," Londono grumbled.

Paige raised an eyebrow and again looked in the mirror. As she and I exchanged glances, her phone rang once more. "Why do I recognize this number, 555-0116?"

"It's Matt's number," I replied. "He's probably calling you because he couldn't reach me on my phone and was worried."

Paige passed her phone back to me.

"Hey, honey."

"It's been hours since you went down to Miami," Matt said. "You usually text me after an arrest. When you didn't, I got worried. Why aren't you answering your phone?"

"Everything is fine," I said, not wanting to worry him. "It was a very uneventful arrest aside from a broken phone. I'll tell you about it later."

Both, Paige and Londono, looked at me, incredulously.

Matt didn't press for answers. "Okay, if you want, invite Paige over for dinner."

I hung up and passed the phone back to Paige. "Matt's making curry, interested in dinner at our place tonight?"

Londono turned his empty stare back at me. "I'll check my schedule."

CHAPTER 3

A little before one, I strolled into the courtroom where Londono's arraignment was about to begin. Paige was already there, sitting in the first row of bench seats in the gallery behind Robert Mullaney, a young dark haired well dressed Assistant United States Attorney, who exuded confidence.

I sat down next to her and held out my new phone. "Lucky for me, Miami field office just got some new ones in."

Paige was uninterested. She hadn't said more than five words to me since we handed Londono off to the Marshals.

The silent treatment had finally gotten to me. "Want to talk about it?" I quietly asked, watching the two Marshals escort Londono and his nephew into the courtroom.

"Do you have a death wish?" She said in a tone laced with annoyance.

Londono nodded at his attorney, and then fixed his gaze on me, the same as he had done throughout his brother's trial.

"I know. I should have kept my mouth shut."

"Why the hell would you say those things to that monster, knowing what he's capable of? Did you forget about all the stuff he did during Miguel's trial?"

"I couldn't help myself. His arrogant, untouchable attitude upset me."

"It was reckless," she growled. "Londono is responsible for at least a dozen deaths that we know of. If he could get out from under these charges by killing you, I believe he'd do it. He's had people killed for a lot less. So, keep that in mind the next time you decide to verbally spar with him."

ICE Agent Steve Rourk, a handsome, ruggedly built forty-year-old man with dark hair, stepped into our aisle.

To make room for him, Paige slid down the bench. "You're playing with fire. Just remember. I warned you."

Steve stroked his goatee and motioned toward the other side of the courtroom, where Eduardo Londono sat next to Miami defense attorney Alian Diaz, an attractive, dark-skinned man in his early forties with a reputation for defending drug dealers. "The only thing that would make this picture more perfect would be to see Londono in a prison orange jump suit."

Paige nodded in agreement and watched the magistrate enter. After the bailiff called the court to order, Judge Ferguson addressed Mr. Diaz. "How do the defendants plead?"

Diaz stood. "Not guilty, Your Honor."

The judge glanced at the defendants. "Considering the severity of the charges under the Continuing Criminal Enterprise statute, bail is denied. We will schedule the Preliminary Hearing for October 7th."

As the Marshals took the pair away, Diaz called out to Londono, "Eduardo, I'll go before another judge and get you bonded out."

Exiting the courtroom, Londono looked over his shoulder and smirked at me. Stunned at his audacity, I nudged Paige. "Did you see that? Can I be arrested for flipping him the bird?"

"I wouldn't do it. If your aim is not perfect the Magistrate may think that you meant it for him. Besides, I don't think you want to antagonize Londono any more than you already have."

"Oh no, what'd she do?" Steve asked.

"She said some things to Londono she shouldn't have on the ride over," Paige replied. "If she ends up dead in the

Everglades, we'll know who ordered the hit."

Steve shook his head in disbelief. "Yep, we just won't be able to prove it and Londono will get away with yet another egregious act." Steve glared at me. "Listen to Paige, otherwise that brash confidence of yours is going to get you into trouble."

"That's hard to do knowing that Rafael and others died because of Londono." With my chin, I motioned toward the AUSA. "I told Mullaney it was too dangerous, that Londono would smell a trap and that I could make the case without Rafael getting Londono on tape discussing the scheme, but *NO* he wanted a slam-dunk of a case."

"Shh." Paige touched my arm as Mullaney stomped past us, and out of the courtroom. We followed him down a corridor to a small, empty conference room we had used earlier in the day.

Mullaney, who Steve frequently referred to as Mussolaney because of the way he ordered people around, tossed his briefcase on the tiny wooden table in the center of the room. "Paige, prep any remaining witnesses, and I will schedule them to go before the standing Grand Jury." Mullaney rubbed his temple. "The cooperator's information was supposed to have been current and accurate. I had anticipated a twenty kilo seizure."

"It was current," Paige said. "Londono must have sold most of the load to his distributers as soon as he got it, bypassing his stash houses. That's probably why he set up that meeting with Rafael."

"How much time will he serve for five kilos?" I asked.

Mullaney tapped his fingers on the tabletop. "Not enough. You and Steve do more research on the port workers and Londono's girlfriend, Rosa Hernandez. See who we can leverage for information. The shipments aren't going to stop just because Londono is behind bars. Theo Rojas, his second in command, will take over and I want to be ready to arrest him when the next shipment comes in." Mullaney pulled his phone from his pocket, pushed a few buttons, held it to his ear, and exited the room. As the door closed behind him, Steve stood at attention and saluted. Paige and I couldn't help but chuckle.

Outside the courthouse, I spotted Alian Diaz standing in the shade across the street. It appeared that he had been waiting for us. Word on the street was that Diaz would do anything to get a client off, including paying witnesses to recant their stories.

As we walked to our cars, Diaz approached. Smoking a cigarette and holding his cell phone up to his ear, he stared at me as if he wanted to say something. I slowed my pace, thinking he was going to stop, but he didn't. He just smirked and walked past.

Steve unlocked his car and glanced over his shoulder at Diaz. "What the hell was that all about?"

Paige gave me a, "I-told-you-so look" and we got into her car.

I waved at Steve as he drove off. "You stopping by the house?"

Paige pulled onto the interstate and headed south toward the PNC bank where I had left my car early that morning. "No, I promised the kids pizza tonight, maybe this weekend. Although, after the looks Londono and Diaz gave you, I don't know that it's safe to be anywhere near you."

In the bank parking lot, I rummaged through my pockets for my car keys. "You think I put a target on my back?"

Paige didn't answer. She just raised her eyebrows.

"Okay, well, let me know what you decide. Matt leaves in the morning and won't be home until Saturday night. He's got to check on the progress of the Atlanta house."

"You think you'll be happy up there? That's Bible Belt country."

I sighed. "Matt's tired of commuting. He wants to work from where he's based, and I understand that."

"It's no South Florida."

I chuckled. "No, but marriage is a compromise. Besides, I want to see Matt more than a few nights a week, and this move is the only way that is going to happen."

Paige nodded. "I understand. By the way, I'm sorry for saying Matt's number out loud."

"Don't worry about it. I think Londono has a lot more on his mind than my husband's phone number."

As soon as I pulled out of the parking lot, my phone rang. It was Steve. "Watch your back. That fierce look from Diaz was probably a message from Londono."

"Yes, I have no doubt his attorney will try to find a way to derail my money laundering case. But, without the restaurants records, which I have locked away in the office, they won't know which vendors Rafael paid off until it's too late to threaten or bribe those people. That's why Mullaney wants to make sure everyone testifies before the Grand Jury before we have to turn over those documents to the defense in Discovery."

"Okay, then I'll get with you tomorrow to plan our strategy regarding Rosa."

"Sounds good." I veered onto Interstate 95, and headed home. Stuck in rush-hour traffic, I reflected on Miguel's trial, all the pressure on the task force, and especially me, to take down the cartel's low-hanging fruit, even if we couldn't get the kingpin himself. It was a long high profile case with the media spotlight on everything, except the hang up and threatening phone calls I had received. When the jury returned a guilty verdict, I was relieved, but also concerned about the repercussions.

I shook those thoughts out of my head. *Nothing happened then, and nothing will happen now.*

17

CHAPTER 4

I pulled into our garage and parked next to Matt's Audi. I wondered if Londono was cunning enough to memorize Matt's number, and if so, just how much information he could obtain by researching it.

As a law enforcement officer, none of my personal information, including purchased properties, was available in public records, but what about Matt's information? Hopefully he had provided the address of his parents' condo back when he was issued his driver's license, and more importantly, when he signed up with his cell phone carrier.

I walked into the house and smelled the delicious aroma of cardamom, coriander, and tamarind, and all my concerns vanished.

"Hey, babe, I'm in the kitchen," Matt called out, stirring a large pot of Indian Curry. "It's spicier than I had planned, but I've got plenty of this." He held up a bottle of beer.

I gave him a kiss, and watched him toss the perfect combination of spices into the simmering concoction on the stove. "How was your day?"

In a loving gesture, Matt ran his free hand up and down my back. "Great. I did some yard work, hit some golf balls, and now my beautiful wife is home."

Quite the charmer, he always said the right things.

I took a drink of his beer. "Say, do you happen to remember what address you provided to your cell phone carrier?"

He tasted his sauce and added more cumin. "No. Why?"

"Just wondering." I grabbed a bottle of water from the refrigerator and strolled out of the kitchen. "If dinner isn't

18

going to be ready for a while, I'm going to do some work on the computer."

"Take all the time you want," Matt called over his shoulder. "And look at the pictures I emailed you of the Atlanta house. It's really coming together."

Seated at the desk in our home office, I wondered if I should mention the phone number incident. Matt was so relaxed and happy. Why cause him to worry about a potential issue that would most likely never come to be. At least I hoped it was a mute issue.

An hour later, Matt poked his head into the office. "Dinner is ready and if we hurry we can catch the sun setting over the lake."

Three years earlier, and just weeks before I joined the HIDTA task force, construction began on our current home located on a large lake lot in Parkland, Florida. That led to a rocky time in our marriage.

Matt had promised to oversee the construction of the new home, but he had just been made captain and was never around to do that. I too was busy. Eager to prove my worth to my new supervisor, that meant working nights, and weekends.

Whenever possible, I would visit the construction site, spot mistakes, and tell Matt about it during our nightly phone conversations.

Matt would get defensive and say, "I can't be there. What do you want me to do about it? I have no seniority when bidding for flights, that means I get those flights with the most legs each day and the ones that have me away from home four days a week."

He also hated coming home only to fight with me and the contractors on the few days he had off work. The project had become a point of contention, and both of us were beyond happy when it was completed.

To avoid similar incidents with the Newnan house, Matt would go to Atlanta a day before his scheduled trip and stay a day afterwards to oversee construction on a weekly basis.

As the sun set over the lake, Matt served up the Chicken Tikka Masala. "Someone from the design team left me a message that the grout color for the kitchen tile had been discontinued."

I gazed out at the orange horizon and tore off a piece of Naan bread. "Can you meet with them and find a color closest to the original?"

Matt nodded in agreement. "Got it scheduled for next week. I'm also putting a note on the employee bulletin board to see if any pilots want to rent the guest bedrooms. That will help us with the mortgage until we get this place sold."

I took a beer from a small metal bucket of ice on the table. "I'll put in for a transfer right away, but I can't leave until after this case goes to trial a few months from now."

Matt pushed his empty plate aside. "Are you going to be alright leaving the task force?"

I scoffed. "Sure. Over the last few years I have seen just how ruthless this Colombian drug cartel can be. And after everything that has happened recently, I look forward to moving to Atlanta and again working white collar crime, or any case where the criminals are not as cold blooded as they are down here."

After I had deposited the dirty plates in the sink, Matt playfully backed me out of the kitchen and into the bedroom. Our long deep passionate kisses set me on fire, that was until his cell phone vibrated across the dresser. Matt rarely received calls at night.

My heart skipped a beat. I glanced over at the phone but was unable to see the display. "You going to get that?"

"Not a chance," he said in a low, sexy voice, as he eased me onto the bed.

We made love, and even with my concerns about the phone call, the sex was amazing as always and there was never any lack of it, even during the tough times. We were lucky. We had both passion and love.

Afterwards, feeling totally relaxed, I got up and sauntered toward the bathroom. Matt's phone vibrated again. The hair stood up on the back of my neck. I couldn't help myself. I grabbed the phone up and looked at the display. The call was from a blocked number.

"Who is this?" I demanded.

Matt sat straight up in bed, his mouth agape.

On the other end of the phone, I heard breathing, then the caller hung up.

CHAPTER 5

As soon as I arrived at work, the next morning, I sprinted across the task force office to my desk. I accessed the ChoicePoint background check database. When the search screen popped up, I typed in Matt's phone number, inhaled deeply, and hit enter.

Prior to Londono's arrest, I had never paid much attention to Matt's incoming calls. On the evenings he was home, Matt rarely got any phone calls, other than the occasional call from crew scheduling or a pilot friend. So, a call from a blocked number was highly unusual.

Like many men, Matt spent a lot of time on his cell phone; reading the news, following the stock market, and watching funny YouTube videos. The only time it had ever bothered me was months earlier when we were having a romantic dinner at Fleming's Steakhouse. Couples were laughing and chatting, but I felt sad. It seemed that Matt was more interested in playing on his phone than having a conversation with me. Had seven years of marriage left us indifferent to each other?

"I feel like I'm dining alone," I told him. "I thought we came out to talk, and enjoy each others company."

That night Matt promptly tucked his phone away and never brought it out again during a meal.

The first page of the background report popped up. I straightened my posture and scrolled to the next screen which listed Matt's parent's address, and that which I had feared the most, our current address. A wave of nausea churned deep in my stomach. Londono could have had his attorney research Matt's phone number to arrive at the same alarming results that I was staring at.

I rested my elbows on the desk and rubbed my

temples. I would have to tell Matt what had happened, but was not looking forward to that conversation. Undoubtedly, Matt will be upset. Who could blame him? Calls from a sadistic drug kingpin who has a vendetta against me and knows where we live is not exactly what Matt had signed up for when we were married.

Eight years earlier, when Matt and I had met at a party on Ft. Lauderdale Beach, I was working white-collar crime, which rarely involved murder. Our meeting was a brief romantic encounter that ended happily-ever-after, like in the movies. It was a warm, balmy night and we spent the entire evening walking along the shore chatting. I remember how attracted I was to him and how he made me laugh. I was reluctant to tell him that I was a Special Agent with IRS Criminal Investigation because I had heard rumors about airline pilots disliking the IRS because they were always getting audited. I avoided telling Matt the whole truth about what I did for a living. I told him a half-truth; that I was an accountant.

Matt had just been hired by Eastern Airlines and was leaving for California the next morning. He had planned to visit his family for two weeks before returning to Florida to begin his new career in Orlando, Florida, three hours north of Ft. Lauderdale. Because we lived in different cities, I doubted that I would ever see him again, so why tell him too much about myself.

Two weeks later, a dozen long-stem red roses were delivered to my office with an invitation to dinner. It turned out that Matt had asked my friend about me and had no problem dating what many men saw as their worst nightmare; a female accountant with a gun. Nor did he have an issue with a long-distance relationship. So, for six months we commuted back and forth, until fate stepped in and he was transferred to Ft. Lauderdale.

***

That evening, when I arrived home, a hungry black cat was waiting for me. I rubbed the cat's head. "Weezer, should I deliver some bad news to Matt over the phone or wait until he returns home at the end of the week?" Weezer just rolled on his back and purred.

After feeding the cat, I retired to the patio with a glass of wine to decide how best to proceed. My first thought was to call Paige. No, she would feel awful to hear that something had come from her slip-up, and I didn't want that. Nor could I talk to my HIDTA Supervisor, James Szish. That would throw Paige under the bus for a mistake anyone could have made. I decided to just tell Matt what had happened so he would be alert to any calls asking him for personal information and so he could be vigilant to suspicious persons in our neighborhood.

My cell phone rang. It was Matt. "Hey babe, are you done flying for the day?"

"Yep, I'm at a nice Hilton hotel in Canton, Ohio. How about you, how was your day?"

I swallowed hard. "I have something to tell you, and I don't know if I should just blurt it out or wait until you get home to discuss it with you."

"Now, you're scaring me. Just tell me. I can't have what ever it is weighing on my mind until Saturday."

I took a long drink of wine. "The guy I arrested knows your telephone number."

There was a long silence on the other end of the phone. "Is that why you've been policing my calls?"

Wow, such harsh words. "More like being aware of your incoming calls," I replied in a rather combative tone.

"Yeah, right," Matt growled. "As far as I'm concerned, the blocked calls I receive are from telemarketers, and I don't answer them. Why would he call my number, why not call you directly?

I tried to keep the tremor out of my voice. "It's a warning. Remember when I asked you about the address you provided to your cell phone carrier? Well, I researched it and from your phone number I was able to find our home address."

"Jennifer, you can look on the iphone lease agreement. I know I didn't give them our address."

Whenever Matt used my full name, he was angry.

"Matt, I'm just telling you what I discovered."

"Well, I'm telling you that our personal information got associated to my phone some other way."

I swiped at the hair, the breeze was blowing in my face. "It doesn't matter how it happened. The problem is that Londono knows where we live."

"He's a drug dealer. Hasn't he been arrested before, probably many times? So, why would he want to harass you, is he known to come after those in law enforcement who do their jobs?"

I got up from the lounge chair and paced the length of the pool. "It's my money laundering case that jammed him up, and if convicted he could be looking at twenty years in prison. So, it's a little more than a slap on the wrist." I paused. "I also put his brother in prison where he recently died."

There was a long silence on the phone.

"So you think he's going to come after you or us?"

"I don't know. I'll discuss it with my supervisor."

Matt cleared his throat. "Are we talking about someone shooting at the house or leaving dead animals at the front door?"

"No, none of that," I chuckled. "I shouldn't have even brought it up. I'm sorry I upset you. I'm telling you this because I want you to be alert to any unusual phone calls or things you see in our neighborhood. I have no idea what Londono will do. Or maybe he'll do nothing at all."

Matt was silent for a long minute. "Let's end this call like this."

That didn't sound good.

"I'll let you know if this Londono person calls me. In the meantime, let's assume that any blocked calls are likely scam calls that I will not answer. I have too many people I would have to reach out to if I were to change my number."

"Matt, I'm not…"

"So, I'm not going to do that. Lastly, I don't want you jumping out of your skin when my phone rings or asking me about every call I receive. I don't do that to you. I trust you. So, I would appreciate it if you offered me the same courtesy. Goodnight."

The phone went dead.

CHAPTER 6

With sunlight in my eyes, and a cat kneading my stomach, I awoke. Or maybe it was because of the rumbling sound of my phone vibrating across the nightstand. I quickly grabbed the phone, thinking it was Matt calling to apologize for how he ended the previous night's conversation. No such luck. It was a message about a mandatory task force meeting at nine o'clock.

The next text was from Paige. *Pick you up in 30.*

Paige pulled into the driveway and I jumped into the passenger seat of her car. "Okay, spill it. What is this meeting about?"

"Good morning to you too, sunshine," she replied. "I'm as clueless as you." She examined the uneasy expression on my face. "What's gotten your panties into such a knot?"

It was time to tell her.

"Matt is receiving calls from a blocked number. He's either having an affair or it's Londono. I'm hoping it's an affair."

"Yeah, an affair would end with a lot less bloodshed." She pounded her hand on the steering wheel. "Damn, it's gotta be Londono. I had hoped he wasn't paying attention to what I had said."

"Yeah, me too. And it gets worse."

Paige laugh-snorted. "How?"

"I did a ChoicePoint search on Matt's number and it listed our current address."

Paige rolled up to a red traffic light. "Wait, if Londono knows your address, he would have no reason to call Matt. He'd just send his thugs over to your house."

"Oh, that very well could happen. I think these first calls are a warning. Matt thinks it's telemarketers. But I'm

27

pretty sure that the FTC prohibits those types of calls after nine at night."

The light turned green and Paige stomped on the gas. "Well, let's hope that Matt's number ended up on some west coast telemarketing list where they're three hours behind us."

At the task force gated parking lot, Paige scanned her entry card, and parked in a shaded spot in front of the five story building. "Tell Mullaney."

"No point to that," I said, exiting the car. "It will be the same as Miguel's trial, burner phones that we are unable to trace."

At the glass door of the building I punched in my access code. We nodded at the armed guard who knew us, and we stepped into the elevator.

"Not true," Paige said. "This time you think Londono has your address and he may be holding a grudge regarding his brother's death."

The elevator opened on the third floor. We followed other task force agents into the conference room and took our seats at the long polished table.

Once Supervisor James Szish, a solidly built forty-year-old man seated next to AUSA Mullaney, saw that everyone was present, he began the meeting. "Last night Orlando Perez's throat was slashed in his home."

Some of the agents appeared surprised, others not so much. After all, Orlando was a member of a drug cartel, and longevity of members was very short lived.

Mullaney impatiently took over. "I'm gonna be blunt." He stared squarely at Steve, with whom he has had run-ins over operational strategies in the past. "Only the people in this room knew that we had the *now deceased* port worker cooperating with us." He turned his focus to me. "Now, once again, our cooperator has been killed."

Incensed, I desperately wanted to shout, "Rafael's death is on you." Instead, I held my tongue.

Steve, however, who could never be accused of not speaking his mind, and who frequently referred to Mullaney as a haughty rising star within the U.S. Attorney's Office, spoke up. "You've got some nerve if you think the leak came from someone in the task force. For all we know, that dumbass told Londono he was jammed up and tried to extort money for his silence."

Mullaney glared at Steve. "If that's the case, find someone who will tell us that's what happened. The bottom line is that I want answers and if you can't get them for me, I'm going to look internally."

"What does that mean?" ICE Agent Jim Paterson demanded.

Szish interjected in a calmer tone. "It means that all of your work product will have to be locked in file cabinets while people comb through our office looking for listening devices. It means that there may be a tap on our phones, or worse case scenario, everyone in this room will be subject to a polygraph exam because the Justice Department suspects that information is being disseminated to someone outside of the task force."

We all knew that an intelligence leak would compromise three long years of work and scrutinize each person's allegiance. The room became dead silent. It was as if Szish had placed a vial of nitroglycerin in the center of the table, and the slightest sound or movement would cause a massive explosion.

"I don't believe this." Neal Phillips finally commented. "The cartel able to bug a secure location. Is that even possible?"

"Sure," Steve replied. "They've done it before. Phone taps, corrupt officials, welcome to South Florida. Where you been, son?"

Mullaney addressed Paige. "Orlando told us that Londono set his girlfriend, Rosa Hernandez, up with an oceanfront condo so she could alert him when a particular ship carrying the drugs had arrived. Has there been any communication between those two?"

"Only one call, in which Londono told Rosa not to come to the jail, that he didn't want her to see him behind bars."

ICE Agent Ryan Dees scoffed. "Yeah right, he doesn't want his wife to run into her."

Paige continued on. "He suggested that she take a vacation, go to the Bahamas for the weekend. She's booked on a flight tomorrow."

"That sounds like he's telling her to take money off shore," Phillips commented.

Steve shook his head. "Not likely. She's taken two trips to Grand Bahama in the past month. Customs searched her as she left the U.S. and returned. Short of conducting a cavity search, they found nothing. Authorities in Grand Bahama reported that she did nothing but lounge around the pool at her hotel."

Mullaney stared at the cartel flowchart on the wall. "Stay on the couriers and the port in case Londono has a shipment in transit."

Szish looked at the faces at the table. "Questions, comments? Okay dismissed."

Chairs scraped back, notebooks flipped shut, and everyone began to leave.

"Jennifer, Steve, hold up," Mullaney said, watching the other agents exit the room. "Last year Paige and Neal approached Rosa. She wouldn't talk with them, but now with Londono's arrest, I think we should take another run at her. Tactfully let her know that willful blindness is not a viable defense."

Steve shrugged. "What could it hurt?"

I nodded in agreement and followed Steve to his cubicle. "I have an idea. Matt flies to Grand Bahama every few weeks. His airline just picked up that route. Rosa doesn't know me. You said she leaves tomorrow. I can fly there for free on Matt's airline and do some surveillance. Think I should run it past Mullaney?"

    Steve chuckled. "Not if you want it to be approved."

***

I arrived home at 6:30 to find a lovely bunch of pink Gladiolas on the kitchen counter. I dropped my purse on the bed, heard the shower running, and tapped on the bathroom door. "Matt, I'm home."

    "I'll be out in a minute. That pilot I told you about, Gary, well he and I played golf. I wanted to clean up. I'm all sweaty."

    "Okay, I'm going stick my feet in the pool."

    "I'll join you in a minute."

    I placed my weapon in the top drawer of the bedside table and saw Matt's phone vibrating across the bed. Before I could see the caller ID, the call went to voice mail. I tried to retrieve the call, but couldn't open the phone. It had been password protected. Apparently, that stunt of rudely answering his phone the other night caused Matt to ensure it wouldn't happen again. So, I gathered up the phone and took it into the bathroom. "Gary may have left something important in your car. Your phone was just ringing and there are two new messages."

    Matt turned off the shower. "I'll call him back as soon as I dry off."

    I heard our home phone ringing and stepped out of the bathroom. "Now, it sounds like he's trying to reach you on our home phone. I'll tell him you're in the shower."

    "Just ignore it," Matt called out. "He wants to go drinking."

    In the kitchen, I took the handset from the wall mount. "Hello?"

No answer.

There was also no caller ID. A moment later, a voice-mail alert appeared on the screen. I retrieved the message only to hear a faint, rhythmic sound; breathing.

"Was it Gary?" Matt appeared behind me with a towel wrapped around his waist.

My blood boiled. "Not unless he has a blocked number."

I walked into our home office to see two messages on the answering machine. I hit the play button and the machine's mechanical male voice said, "Call number one." There was silence, and the call ended. It was the same for the second message.

Matt looked blankly at me. "You think those are from that guy you arrested?"

I walked numbly into the kitchen. Matt followed and pulled a bottle of wine from the refrigerator.

I struggled to keep my emotions in check. "He killed another informant last night. So yes, I know those calls are from him. Another warning."

A shadow crossed Matt's face. There was something he wasn't telling me. "Matt, have you received any strange calls or calls from the man I arrested?"

Matt finished pouring his glass of wine and took a drink. "No."

"I need to know if you have. This is serious. I need to tell the AUSA. What Londono is doing is harassment."

"I told you, I haven't." His phone vibrated on the kitchen counter. Matt gazed at the screen. "Damn it. Gary again. Let me get rid of him."

He stomped into the bedroom, sat on the bed, and in an irritated tone said to his friend, "Listen, I can't meet you out for a drink tonight."

I padded into our home office. What was Londono up to? A minute later, Matt joined me. "I agreed to meet Gary

32

tomorrow for lunch. He's having a tough time. His live-in girlfriend left him."

"That's too bad," I replied, gazing at the credit card statement in my hand.

Matt stepped behind me and rubbed my tense shoulders. "Jenn, I haven't received any hang up or threatening calls. If it would help, why don't we get rid of the home phone? We each have cell phones. I can have it disconnected tomorrow."

"Yes, thank you, do that." I paused. "Hey, quick question. How easy would it be for you to get me a seat on your airline to Grand Bahama tomorrow?"

"Near impossible. Since we started servicing the Bahamas, the flights have been over booked. Why?"

"I wanted to check something out for work. It was just a thought." I again turned my attention back to the credit card statement. "Oh, and if you want to surprise me with something, I suggest you don't charge it to the credit card."

Matt looked perplexed. "What are you talking about?"

I held up the statement. "$365, Hawks Cay Resort."

Matt raked his hand through his hair. "Damn, I meant to tell you about that. I'm sorry to disappoint, but it's not for us. The co-pilot I was flying with wanted to grab the last room at that price and didn't have a credit card on him. So, I put it on our card."

"What?"

"It was just to hold the room. He'll pay cash when he arrives and it will get backed off our card."

"And what if it isn't removed from our card?"

"It will be. I know where to find the guy. I fly with him all the time." Matt meandered out of the office.

Strange, I thought. Who doesn't carry a credit card?

CHAPTER 7

Seated behind the wheel of his car devouring a turkey sub, Steve said, "According to Mullaney, the preliminary hearing went well, even without Orlando's testimony."

I nodded. "I can't believe Mullaney and the defense agreed to the December 15th trial date."

"Sure, why not? Aside from Rosa, we have as much as we're going to get and if Diaz were to push it back to January, well, that's all the longer that Londono would be sitting in jail. By the way, did Mullaney put the kabash on your idea about spying on Rosa in the Bahamas?"

I swallowed a mouthful of ham on rye. "I never spoke to him about it. Matt said the flights were overbooked and I could get stranded there. Maybe Rosa's in the same boat. After all, we've been sitting out here for hours."

Steve turned the radio dial from music to a sports talk channel. "Nope, she's back. I looked at the Customs report before I dragged you out here. She returned home yesterday. Let's just give it another hour before we leave."

He took a long gulp of soda, contorted his face, and passed the drink to me. "Here, I think this one is diet."

The garage door slowly opened and a Mercedes SUV zipped up the driveway.

Steve and I jumped from our car and sprinted up the driveway.

"Cuando Me Enamoro" blasted from the SUV's radio. With her back to us, Rosa leaned into the vehicle, and gathered up packages from the passenger seat.

I caught Steve admiring the shapely black haired beauty's ass.

Rosa gasped when she saw us, and the carefree expression on her face immediately disappeared when we presented our badges.

"Ms. Hernandez, my name is Jennifer Weber. I'm with Criminal Investigation of the IRS and this is Agent Steve Rourk with Immigration and Customs Enforcement. We have a few questions we'd like to ask you."

Rosa's large, dark brown eyes glared at me, as if sizing me up. Londono must have mentioned my name based on the daggers coming from Rosa's stare. She slammed the SUV door shut and defensively asked, "What do you want?"

Steve, a handsome, confident man, generally has good luck when it comes to encouraging people of the female persuasion to open up to him, so I let him begin the dialogue.

"Ms. Hernandez, we know that you are an associate of Eduardo Londono and ...."

Steve didn't even get out of the gate before Rosa rudely interrupted. "I don't know what you mean by associate. He is a family friend."

Steve held up his hand. "Please let me finish. We've met with Mr. Londono and his attorney numerous times. We know exactly what he is. We're here to offer you the opportunity to tell us what you know about his business, and in exchange we will make arrangements for you and your family to enter into the U.S. Marshals Witness Protection Program."

Rosa again tried to interrupt, but this time Steve shut her down by loudly plowing on. "It's too late to proclaim your innocence. You and I both know that Londono's business is drug trafficking."

A flabbergasted Rosa glanced at me, then back at Steve. "I don't know anything of the sort."

The conversation went back and forth like a tennis match. Then it was Steve's volley. "We also know that you, along with others, help Londono launder his drug proceeds.

So, the deal I am offering you, one parent to another, is the opportunity to continue to be a mother to your two children."

In an attempt to appeal to Steve's libido, Rosa tilted her head, seductively looked up at him, and in her best flirty demure voice, said, "But, I really don't know anything and don't want to be involved."

I think she even batted her long, dark eyelashes at him.

But good old Steve came right back at her. "Well, you are involved, and this is your opportunity to help yourself."

Since Steve wasn't making much progress, I stepped in. "Ms. Hernandez, where are you currently employed?"

Rosa looked at Steve as if he could help her answer the question. "Uh, at a real estate company."

"And what do you do at this real estate company?" I asked.

Shifting her weight from one sexy stiletto high heel to the other, in a hostile defensive tone, she replied, "I'm the receptionist. Why?"

That was the exact response I wanted. I went in for the verbal kill. "Well, for a receptionist making sixteen hundred dollars a month, how do you afford rent on this lovely house, a private school for your children, and the lease on that vehicle?"

That really set Rosa off. She went from defensive to confrontational in a matter of seconds. "Eduardo and my family help me out. But, that doesn't mean that I know anything about his business."

I forged on, knowing what needed to be said. "Based on my calculations and your lifestyle, it seems like you receive help to the tune of approximately four thousand dollars each month. You and I both know the money you receive is from illegal drug proceeds, and when I prove it, you will be imprisoned for a very long time."

Rosa snapped. "I want you to leave *now!*" emphasizing the word now.

I nodded in agreement, but had one last thought-provoking bomb to drop before departing. "Fine, but is your seventy-two-year-old mother going to be able to raise your five-year-old and eight-year-old children while you're in jail? Or do you want to see your mother go to prison? Because it looks like she lives here too, so I'm sure she knows what's been going on, especially regarding the rent on this place." I paused. "Think about that because my next focus will be on the money running through her bank account."

Not yet receiving the mother's bank records, I had to ad-lib. But it must have touched a nerve because Rosa flipped. "How dare you threaten my family! Get out! Leave me alone!"

I placed my business card on the hood of the SUV before exiting the garage. Wanting to have the last word, I glanced over my shoulder and pleasantly added, "Call us if you change your mind."

Rosa flipped me off and yelled, "Puta!"

Steve got in the car and chuckled. "I think she had the last word, and if my Spanish is correct, it wasn't a very nice one."

He pulled the car away from Rosa's house and hopped on Interstate 95 heading north. "You were an excellent bad cop. That thing about her mother was a nice touch. That really pissed her off." Steve shook his head. "She sure is a beauty. It's hard to imagine such a hot chic with that old fart we have sitting in jail."

"Women like her are trouble." I took a sip of diluted diet Pepsi. "She uses her good looks to get what she wants, money. When that dries up, she'll move on to the next sucker. But hey, we should get some good chatter on the wire, now."

***

At nine o'clock that night, I heard someone knocking on my front door. I grabbed my gun from the nightstand and peered through the peep hole. Paige stood there with a bleak look on her face.

I opened the door. "What's going on?"

"We need to talk." She followed me into the kitchen.

"Matt's on a trip," I opened the refrigerator. "I'll get us some wine. Looks like you need it."

I poured each of us a glass of white wine and waited. Paige pushed her glass back to me. "You're going to need this more than me."

She hiked herself up onto a high top stool at the kitchen counter. "You know that we're listening to all of Londono's jail house calls. Right? Well, this evening he called Rosa."

"Steve and I paid a visit to Rosa today. She probably had quite a bit to say."

"She did. Rosa told Londono that she wanted to have you killed."

"What?"

Paige took her glass of wine back and took a sip. "I don't think that Londono is foolish enough to order a hit on a federal agent because his irate girlfriend tells him to."

"I wouldn't count on that. Londono hates me. What did he say?"

"He tried to calm her down and told her she was saying way too much over the phone. He knows we're listening to his calls. He asked her to visit him tomorrow." Paige shrugged her shoulders. "I don't think he'll do anything, but hey, what do I know?"

She stood up and grabbed her purse from the back of the stool. "I have to get home to my kids. I left a message for Mullaney. I'll wait to see how he wants to proceed." She held up her glass in a toast. "Hey, nice shit bomb you ignited."

CHAPTER 8

Once agents were seated at the conference room table, Mullaney kicked off the morning briefing, glaring over at Steve. "I listened to Londono's conversation with Rosa. It seems that my suggestion for you to tactfully let her know that willful blindness is not a viable defense, didn't go over very well."

Some agents chuckled, and Steve loudly scoffed. "That's an understatement."

Mullaney turned his undaunted gaze on me. "It would be stupid for Londono to go after you, and he is anything but stupid. However, that said. I don't want to take any chances, so I have requested that you have police protection."

I stared at him with disdain, knowing he would have handled the situation differently, privately, if I were a man. I rested my forearms on the tabletop and leaned in. "I don't want protection. Like all the gun carrying male agents and police in this room, I can protect myself."

Mullaney looked at Szish, who shrugged. "Okay, but if we hear anything that indicates that Londono is going to take action, you will have no choice in the matter."

I nodded, "understood."

Szish added one last thing. "Until this blows over, I think we should curtail your field interviews and conduct all trial prep here or at the U.S. Attorney's Office."

The meeting adjourned.

I wondered why Rosa wanted to have me killed? That was my first encounter with her. It had to have been something that I said. A tell in poker is a change in a person's attitude or behavior. Rosa's tell pertained to her mother. Note to self, pull all her mother's bank information.

I exited the conference room alongside Joel Chase, a handsome Ft. Lauderdale Police Officer who looked younger than his thirty-six years. "Hi, haven't seen much of you lately."

Chase nodded and walked with me to my cubicle. "Surveillance, I took evenings while I'm waiting to receive the phone records that I subpoenaed." He paused in the corridor outside my cubicle. "So, the Crab Shack your new happy hour spot?"

"What are you talking about?"

"The night before Londono's arrest."

I eased into my chair and booted up my computer. "I'm confused. You think you saw me there?"

"Well, not you, but Matt. I just assumed you were with him."

Three years on a drug task force resulted in lots of parties and drinks at bars as a group. Girlfriends, wives, and husbands occasionally joined in, and that's how Joel became acquainted with Matt. They also occasionally golfed together.

"Across from Embassy Suites on 17th Street?"

"Forget it." Joel turned to walk away. "I only caught a glimpse for a minute."

Curiosity got the better of me. "No wait. What did you see?"

He kept walking. "I shouldn't have said anything."

I followed and grabbed his arm to stop him. "What are you talking about? Do you know something you're not telling me?" I expected him to say no.

"Yes."

My heart stopped beating for a moment. "Tell me."

He exhaled loudly. "I spotted a person I thought was Matt walking into the Crab Shack behind a woman. I thought you were with them, ahead of them. I was parked a ways back on surveillance. The money courier I was following went to that Mexican restaurant in the same plaza as the Crab Shack."

Concerned, I thought about it for a minute. "The night before the arrest?"

Joel nodded.

Then it came to me, along with a wave of relief, and I said, "Matt was away on a trip and didn't return home until late, like eleven."

Joel shrugged. "A case of mistaken identity. It was six when I was out there. I shouldn't have said anything."

***

After work, I walked into the house, and heard the Beatles song "Yesterday" softly playing. Slouched in a chair on the patio, with his feet up on the table and a beer in his hand, Matt was talking on his cell phone. He saw me, ended his conversation, and came inside.

Always the romantic, he took me in his arms and started slow dancing. "My trip got cancelled. So, you have me all to yourself for the next few days and from the look on your face, it appears that you need that."

Even on my worst day, Matt could coax a smile to my lips. Nuzzling my ear, he whispered, "What's going on?"

Lost in the gentle swaying motion of the dance and Matt's strong protective arms, I cast the day's events from my mind. To tell him what Londono's crazy girlfriend did would only upset him. Matt was a fixer. There was rarely a repair he couldn't handle around the house or a work dilemma he wasn't prepared to resolve. But the Londono situation was entirely different.

"Joel thought he saw you at the Crab Shack the night before I arrested Londono."

Matt twirled me. "I've been told that we all look alike in uniform, and airline crews do stay at the Embassy Suites across from there." He pulled me close and whispered in my ear. "I'm making Shepherd's Pie for dinner, but I can't find any cheddar cheese."

"Bottom right bin."

Matt dipped me and ended our dance. "Besides, I know better than to go there without bringing you home a container of their clam chowder." He gave me a peck on the cheek and pulled his work schedule from a kitchen drawer. "This is not going to brighten your mood."

"Let me guess, one weekend off," I said despondently while scanning the document.

Theatrically sprinkling cheese over his meat and potato creation, Matt kissed his fingertips and placed the casserole in the oven. "Voilà. You said you'd be preparing for trial, so I didn't think you'd be terribly upset. It also gives me time to get things done at the Atlanta house."

Matt meandered into the bedroom.

I followed him, still reviewing his schedule. "Mostly week days off." I commented, watching him slip into swim trunks.

"Sorry, nothing I can do about it. But, on a positive note, dinner will be ready in thirty minutes. Until then, I will be in the pool, if you'd like to join me."

"No, I want to get some work done before dinner."

I walked into the garage to retrieve case files from my car. Glancing down the driveway, I noticed a piece of paper hanging from the mailbox. I walked down the drive and reached into the mailbox.

At that exact moment, I heard the screech of tires. My head snapped up. Out of nowhere, a car whipped around the corner. I gasped. The mail in my hand fell to the ground. I glanced around, looking for cover. Exposed, with nothing except a skinny palm tree nearby, I pulled my weapon out from under my jacket.

A blue car shot toward me. Gripping my weapon, about to take aim, I glared through the windshield. My brain numbly registered the driver. He was a young long-haired male, oblivious to everything around him, singing along to some hip-hop music blasting from the car radio. I quickly tucked my weapon behind my back and watched the car dart into the neighbor's driveway.

I leaned over and rested my hands on the tops of my legs. *I need to get a grip*, I told myself. I didn't think the Londono thing was affecting me, but obviously, it was.

I grabbed what turned out to be a stinking pressure-cleaning ad hanging from the mailbox and wadded it into a tight ball. As I snatched up the mail I had dropped, I spotted a cigarette butt on the ground, and another one nearby. Surprised to find trash, let alone cigarette butts, on my property, I picked them up, both Marlboro. Had someone parked at the end of my driveway, smoking cigarettes while watching the house?

I joined Matt on the patio where he was doing laps in the pool. "Did you get the mail today?"

Matt stopped swimming. "No, you expecting something?"

I opened my hand and displayed the cigarette butts. "I found these at our mailbox."

Matt climbed out of the pool and briefly inspected the trash I was holding. "Maybe they blew into our yard." He dried off. "Or maybe one of the neighbors smokes when they walk their dog."

I didn't buy it. Once again I thought Londono.

Matt squeezed my shoulder. "Jenn, don't over think this. Isn't it possible that they have been there for a while?"

"No, this is the first time I've ever seen cigarettes at our mailbox, and just like the recent calls we've been receiving, it all started with Londono's arrest."

Matt pulled me into his arms. "I've never seen you like this. I'm concerned."

.

CHAPTER 9

The next morning while I was getting ready for work, Matt waltzed in and happily announced, in an exaggerated Cockney accent, "Breakfast is served." He set a small plate of toast and a cup of coffee on the vanity.

I swiped blush on my cheeks while gazing in the mirror. "So, what are your plans today?"

Matt wrapped his arms around my waist. "I don't know. I'll do things around the house and maybe have lunch with one of the guys. What time do you think you'll be home?"

Taking a bite of toast, I motioned for Matt to follow me into the bedroom, where I holstered my weapon under my jacket. "Hopefully, around 6 o'clock, why?"

"I thought we could have dinner at Laurel and Richard's restaurant," he replied, referring to our neighbor's bay side seafood eatery.

"That sounds great." I looked at the text message from Paige. *Waiting for you in the driveway.*

I kissed Matt goodbye and headed out. After a night of lovemaking, I felt relaxed and carefree, until I got in the car and noticed the sour look on Paige's face. "What now?"

"Mullaney has summoned us to his office and he won't say what it is about," she replied. "If you recall, the last time he called us in without explanation, he told us that our key witness had been murdered."

"That's right, and our entire case was shot to hell. But let's think positive, maybe Londono killed himself."

Then in unison we said, "Nah, too easy."

We arrived at Mullaney's office, and I immediately sensed tension. Steve, visibly upset, asked, "So, exactly when did Rosa say that Jennifer and I grabbed the cocaine that we didn't know was there?"

I was hoping that Steve was once again yanking my chain. That notion swiftly vanished.

"I didn't get details," Mullaney said. "But I think you're missing the bigger issue here. After Londono spoke with the Hernandez woman, the Marshals intercepted another call he made, this time to a suspected cartel associate where he passed along that information."

My jaw dropped. "Holy shit. This guy is relentless."

Mullaney nodded in agreement. "We know that Londono never imports less than twenty kilos at a time. When five were seized at the stash house, I assumed he had sold the rest."

"We all did," Paige replied.

Steve shook his head in disgust. "But instead you're telling us that the girlfriend's place was a stash house containing fifteen kilos of cocaine." He turned to me. "Damn, we were right there. We should've had a search warrant for her place?"

"We had no probable cause," Mullaney retorted.

"What's the street value of fifteen kilos?" Steve asked.

"A million dollars," Paige replied.

Steve raised his eyebrows. "Oh, they'll come looking for that, for sure."

"I don't believe this," I said, looking directly at Mullaney. "After we left Rosa's, we went back to the task force." I turned to Steve. "And I went home about six."

"Yeah, same here," Steve said.

"What about an arrest warrant for Rosa?" I asked. "You have her on tape stating that she had the drugs at her residence?"

Mullaney shook his head. "Any good attorney will have her retract her statement. Claim that she said that to get a rise out of us because she knew we were listening in. Besides, it sounds like the evidence is gone."

I glared at Mullaney. "Okay, then let's take a step back. Who is going to believe Londono's story?"

"I'll tell you who will believe it," Mullaney barked. "The Colombians who want to be paid for the product they shipped over here."

Mullaney got up from his desk and crossed his arms over his chest. "I'm checking on the validity of those calls, and I have a meeting with Londono's attorney this afternoon to get a feel for how much of his client's story he actually believes. I also reached out to DEA and ICE to see if we can get some intel with regard to the cartel sending hit men here to the states, and Customs assured us that they will be extra diligent in monitoring anyone trying to enter the United States from Colombia. I'm telling you this because I inquired about the two of you receiving protection."

"Why would the Colombians bother with the expense of exporting hit men to kill us, when they already have Londono's crew here?" Steve joked. "After all, they're doing a pretty good job of killing off our informants."

"I'm not saying they will do that. I'm just covering all our bases until we get a handle on this," Mullaney replied. "And because of these new allegations, we also have to schedule each of you for a polygraph. So, I suggest that you advise your agency superiors of these developments. They can contact me if they want. In the meantime, stay alert until we figure out what we're dealing with." Mullaney sat back down behind his desk. "Now, if you'll excuse me, I have to brief my chief on this matter."

In the ninth floor lobby, Paige punched the elevator button numerous times. "This case just went from bad to worse. Londono put a target on your backs, and as you know, we're not dealing with your run-of-the-mill criminal here. These guys are a murderous bunch. They don't like law enforcement to begin with. I wouldn't put it past the Colombian who shipped the cocaine to send one of his men here to Florida to check out Londono's story and kill either

Londono or the federal agents that Londono said had ripped off a million dollars worth of cocaine."

We retrieved our weapons from the first floor security lockers. Paige holstered her weapon and quietly said, "You two should never have gone over to Rosa's house."

"Once again, that was Mullaney's bright idea," I retorted.

Steve shook his head as we walked to the parking garage. "I know why she wants Jennifer whacked. What I don't understand is why Rosa would throw me under the bus. I was nice to her. I thought we connected."

I stared at Steve in disbelief.

Paige smirked. "I guess she realized that Londono wasn't going to kill Jennifer, so she found another way of getting rid of her, actually both of you."

"Look, Londono knows that Rosa has the drugs," I said. "He only accused us of taking them so the jury will think that we're dirty cops. Do you really think the Colombians are going to believe Londono? Think about it. They know he's in jail. The money he could get from selling the cocaine would take care of his family while he's gone, or maybe he's going to have Rosa sell the cocaine, so he will have a nice nest egg for the two of them when he gets out. Either way, he and Rosa have one million reasons to keep the drugs or the money and point the finger at us."

Paige unlocked her car. "I agree. The problem is that the person in Colombia has been doing business with Londono for many years, without incident. Then this happens. What you have to consider is that the police in Colombia are corrupt, so the trafficker probably thinks that American cops are just as crooked as their own people."

Steve leaned against the side of his car. "They also only know what they read in the papers, and what the media reported was that five kilos were seized. If they shipped twenty kilos, you can be damn sure they're going to come looking for the other fifteen or their money, and they will make an example of the person or persons who took it. And right now that appears to be us."

PART TWO

RETRIBUTION

CHAPTER 10

The next few weeks went by quickly and without incident. It was December, and Londono's trial was about to begin.

Mullaney had Paige and various task force agents working twelve-hour days organizing exhibits and scheduling witnesses. ICE agent Ryan Dees took over for Steve and some agent from another IRS group was brought in as my replacement.

James Szish had left me a message asking for me to attend a meeting at the task force. Hoping the meeting was to tell Steve and me that DEA had found the missing cocaine, I reached out to Paige for more information.

"Watch out," Paige warned. "I don't think you have to worry about Londono or the cartel as much as you should be concerned about Mullaney. He's been holding a lot of secretive, closed door meetings with people from outside agencies and he advised us not to disclose anything about the case to you. He didn't say don't share with Jenn and Steve, just you."

In the task force break room, standing there with my cell phone glued to my ear, I stared out at the supervisor's closed door. Maybe this wasn't so much a resolution, as it was an execution.

"There's no way they can think that you're in league with that drug dealer." Matt said with conviction.

I gazed up at the ceiling, consumed with fear-induced denial. "Londono is so calculating. Every move this guy makes is deliberate and always one step ahead of us."

"That accusation was just an attempt to discredit you and Steve. The government attorney has to realize that?"

The supervisor's door opened. I turned and poured coffee into my empty mug. "I have to go."

"I love you. Call me later," Matt said.

AUSA Mullaney glared at me from a distance. My stomach sank. That can't be good.

As expected, within minutes of settling back behind my desk, the phone rang. I was summoned to Supervisor James Szish's office.

Szish had the usual serious default expression on his face. "Close the door."

I eased myself into one of the two chairs in front of his desk. The cushion on the chair was still warm from where Mullaney sat and probably bolstered his recommendation for both Steve and me to be removed from the case. But what came next from Szish's mouth was even more of a shock. "Mullaney thinks you're the leak."

I blinked in disbelief. My middle tightened. Just when I thought things couldn't get worse, they did.

Szish glared at me with his blue eyes and an unreadable expression on his clean-shaven face. "Mullaney has initiated a Treasury investigation into your finances."

"Wait. He called in the Treasury Inspector General for Tax Administration, TIGTA?"

Szish gave me a long, penetrating look. "Mullaney, or maybe it was TIGTA, found that you recently had a second home built in Atlanta, Georgia, and that you put a large deposit down with funds coming from an out-of-state bank account in your mother's name."

"Just because drug dealers purchase assets with drug money and claim that it was loaned to them by family members, doesn't mean that I'm doing the same."

Szish nodded in agreement. "Does that mean that TIGTA will find that it was a legitimate loan from your mother?"

"Absolutely," I said, shaking inside and out. Then it occurred to me, Londono could do something to make it appear otherwise. He had far-reaching tentacles in the business world, which included banking.

Szish's tone was like a walk on egg shells where he avoided biting words like murder and mole. "Mullaney thinks you provided Londono with information about Rafael and Orlando. As you know, without them we have a very weak case."

"And based on the assertions Londono has leveled against me and Steve, we have an even weaker case. I'm guessing that Mullaney also suggested that we be reassigned."

Szish furrowed his brow. He didn't like to hear accusations about his agents. All of us had at least five years of law enforcement experience and stellar reputations prior to being selected for the task force. He could not imagine that any one of us would sacrifice our careers for money from Eduardo Londono. However if that was the path that the AUSA wanted to explore, it was Szish's job to make sure everything was done by the book, and no one was being railroaded.

"Just last month, I provided your SAC with a status report citing exemplary work, saying we needed to keep you until this investigation is finished. But, there's no better way to create doubt in the minds of the jurors than dirtying up the investigators."

I sat quietly and waited for the other shoe to drop.

"I'm not ready to throw a dedicated law enforcement officer under the bus because of claims coming from a known criminal. Cooperate fully with TIGTA, take the polygraph, then we'll see where we're at."

I managed a half smile before hearing the other shoe hit the floor.

Szish pushed himself up from behind his desk. "Jennifer, if Mullaney is not happy with the results, he'll be pursuing criminal prosecution."

***

After work, in a trancelike state, I walked into my house and stared out at the lake.

Matt jumped up from the sofa and came to my side. "So, how'd it go?"

"Not good. Mullaney thinks we bought the Atlanta house with drug proceeds and is threatening criminal prosecution."

He wrapped his arms around me and squeezed me tight. "It's unbelievable that your supervisor is going to take the word of some drug dealer."

"It's not Szish. He knows this was a ploy. The problem is it worked. Even if we're cleared of the accusations, Londono's lawyer will bring this up during trial and once it's said the jury won't unhear it."

Matt kissed my forehead. "What can I do?"

My lip trembled. "Nothing. Three years of work on this case. The money laundering portion of it is almost complete. And because Don White wants his IRS group to take credit for this investigation, he has convinced Mullaney to replace me with some kiss-ass agent from his group." I'm silent for a moment. "Even if I pass the polygraph and I'm cleared from wrong doing after the TIGTA investigation, my reputation will be questioned. There will always be rumors or doubt in a co-worker's mind."

I stepped back and took a long swig of Matt's beer. "I'm going to take some time off. How about if I hang out with you up in Atlanta for a few days? I can stay through the closing of our house next week."

Matt grabbed his schedule from the kitchen drawer and looked it over. "I leave tomorrow, have three legs, and an overnight in Wichita, Kansas. Don't think you want to do that. But the next day, I finish early and end up in Atlanta. Why don't you relax tomorrow. Get together with Paige or Julie and fly up the next day."

Matt was referring to Julie Owens, my co-worker and friend at IRS Criminal Investigation. Before I could respond, he had the phone pressed up to his ear, making a reservation at the Marriott. "Hi, yes, I'll hold." Matt wrapped his arms around me. "I hate how it happened, but this works out. We'll both be there for the closing." He stepped back, touched my frowning face, and gave me a compassionate smile.

I pushed out all the anger and fear that had gripped me upon hearing the words criminal prosecution.

How fortunate I was to have a loving partner to help me through the trying times. A wave of relief washed over me. Soon we'd be in our new house. I'd be cleared of any wrong doing, and investigating white collar crime far away from the drama of South Florida.

CUNNING

CHAPTER 11

I exited the jetway at the Atlanta airport feeling better after spending the previous day with Julie, who had convinced me that everything Londono and Rosa had done could and would soon be cleared up.

Paige was in Fort Myers, wrapping up a case she had been working on there.

Matt greeted me with a kiss on the cheek, and motioned toward the pilots and crew exiting my flight, "I'll be right back." He strolled over and briefly chatted with the group while I retrieved a voicemail from Steve. "You were smart getting out of town. I've been placed on admin leave from the task force until my polygraph on Tuesday."

Where was my notification about a polygraph? Had Mullaney postponed it until he had a TIGTA report, so he could prepare a list of incriminating financial questions?

Matt rejoined me, took my carryon roller bag, and proceeded toward the exit. Something was off. Instead of taking my hand, as he usually did even on those humdrum trips to the grocery store, this aloof man beside me was focused on getting to where he was going, and in a hurry.

Had something happened at his work or with construction on the house? In an attempt to be supportive, and find out what was bothering him, I reached over and lovingly took hold of his hand. That lasted all of a minute before he let go and pulled something up on his cell phone. I stopped walking and stepped out of the crowded corridor. Matt continued on for another ten paces before he realized that I was not beside him.

Irritated, I walked up to him and said, "You're dashing along like you're late for a flight. I thought this was going to be a fun, romantic trip."

55

"It will be once I figure out where we have to go to connect with the hotel shuttle."

"Relax. We're in no hurry to get to the hotel." I pointed to a Chili's Grill and Bar ahead of us. "You want to stop for a drink and call the Marriott?"

"No, let's wait til we get to the hotel." He stepped back into the bustle of people and headed toward the escalators.

From the other side of the crowded concourse, a man called out. "Matt, hey."

I could have sworn that I heard Matt let out an irritated moan.

A handsome thirty-something dark haired pilot in uniform walked over. "You just get off work?"

Again, Matt stepped out of the busy concourse. "We came up to close on our house."

The man held his hand out to me. "Is this your wife?"
I smiled. "Yes, Jennifer, and you are?"

"David Frey," he said, and turned to Matt. "When I jumped off the employee bus, I ran into the crew you usually fly with. They were getting on the bus that's heading to the employee lot and out for a drink. You on your way to a crash pad?"

"Nope, staying at the Marriott this weekend," Matt replied. "Don't think Jenn would much like some of the crash pads I've seen."

David stepped back into a swarm of people. "That's true. Good seeing you."

Matt again headed for the tram and said, "Even the trashy crash pads rent for a hundred a month. At our new house I think we can put two twin beds in each bedroom, a dresser, a tv, and ask one fifty or two hundred a month from each person we rent to."

"Sounds good." I wondered if all the preparation for renters was what was troubling him.

Outside of baggage claim, we jumped on a Marriott shuttle. "Four to six hundred a month would really help with the mortgage," he said. "It would be nice to have extra money coming in until we sell the Florida house."

It occurred to me as we entered the Marriott, maybe our financial situation was what had Matt so distracted that he hadn't asked about things with my work.

Once in the room, he flopped on the bed and stared at his phone. "Rather than sit in the hotel bar, let's get a bottle of wine and room service." He pointed out the window. "The view of downtown Atlanta is better from up here."

I gazed out at the downtown high-rise buildings, and laid down next to him to peruse the menu. "Okay, I'll have the Cobb salad." I passed the menu to him. "You seem tired. I'm going to take a bath if you want to nap for a while." I went into the bathroom, and with the water running into the large jacuzzi tub, called out, "You interested in joining me?"

"What? Uh no, I think I'll go downstairs to pick out a bottle of wine." He got up. "They don't have a wine list. So, I'll go to the bar to order our food and pick out the wine while you're in the tub."

After glancing at himself in the mirror, he gave me a peck on the cheek and left. I poked my head out of the room. "Don't forget wine glasses. All we have here are regular drinking glasses."

With a wave and a cheeky backward glance, Matt continued on to the elevator.

I tied my hair up and eased into the hot jacuzzi. I needed to find some way to encourage him to stay off his phone without sounding like a nagging wife.

After watching an entire episode of *Law and Order* on the flat screen television on the wall of the bathroom, I got out of the tub and touched the screen on my phone with shriveled fingers. About to text Matt for an update on our food, he entered the room with a bottle of wine and two glasses.

"You were gone a long time."

He opened the wine, poured a glass, and handed it to me. "Me lady."

I smelled liquor on his breath. "You started without me."

"Jenn, come on. Don't start."

I shrugged and dropped the subject.

"I ran into a couple of guys I trained with and had a beer with them." He walked me over to the window to admire the night skyline. "I told the waiter not to put the food order in until I was ready to leave the bar. I'm sorry. I didn't know you were that hungry. I figured I would leave you to soak while I caught up with my friends. Was that wrong?"

"No, I just didn't expect you to be gone so long." For some odd reason, my thoughts shifted to what Joel had told me.

Matt kissed my neck. "You didn't see my message, did you?"

I looked at my phone and felt silly. *Having a drink with a friend. Back in an hour.*

***

The next morning we met up with our realtor, a lovely forty-year-old woman with blonde hair, and the bluest eyes I have ever seen.

"Jennifer hi, I'm Robin Taggert," she said in a *Gone With the Wind* Georgia accent. It's so nice to finally meet you. How bout I show you folks around the area before we do the walk through and closing of your new home?" Robin pointed to her Explorer. "I can drive."

Matt opened the front passenger door for me. "Why don't you sit up front so you two can talk." He jumped into the back seat.

The majority of the morning, Robin and I chatted about the importance of a nice large kitchen, school ratings, and shopping convenience as she drove us around Peachtree City and the Fayetteville area. When he wasn't playing on his phone, Matt occasionally asked questions about the warranty on the big-ticket items, such as the roof or septic system.

Back in our development, Robin parked in the driveway of a beautifully landscaped two story brick house. "So, what do you think of your new home?"

I stepped out of the car, admiring the wooded area surrounding the property.

Matt pointed at the two large trees in the front yard. "I asked the contractor to save as many trees on our lot as possible."

I wrapped my arms around him. "I love it."

Robin handed Matt the keys to the house. "That first tree is a Magnolia and the one to the left is Oak." She paused, and looked at her phone. "I have some calls I have to return, so I'm going to let you tour the house alone. I'll be in shortly so we can tag any areas you see that need work or a paint touch up."

On the large wraparound porch, I ran my hands over the white railing and hugged Matt as he unlocked the front door. "I can see us sitting in rocking chairs out here sipping mint juleps."

I felt his phone vibrate in his pocket.

He opened the door. "You don't like mint."

I made a face at him. "Okay, a glass of wine."

We walked through the foyer and into the living room. Matt looked at his caller id and shoved his phone back into his pants pocket.

Concerned about Matt's strange behavior the previous day and his obsession with his phone, I asked, "Is everything alright?"

"Yeah, sure, why wouldn't it be?"

I stopped him, stared into his eyes, and asked the one question that no woman should ever expect a truthful response from. "Are you seeing another woman?"

Matt scoffed and walked into the large, open family room connected to the kitchen. "Don't be ridiculous. He showed me Gary's name on the cell phone display and pointed outside. "Look at the dense wooded area past the backyard. Nice isn't it?"

I followed him upstairs into our large master bedroom, where he gazed out the window. "Look at this. Lots of privacy."

I admired the view, wandered into the two guest bedrooms, and headed back downstairs to the kitchen, trying to shake an uncomfortable feeling that was telling me that something was wrong. I didn't know if it was paranoia or fear, or for that matter why it was happening now that I was away from South Florida.

In the kitchen, Matt ran his hands over my arms. "What's going on? You keep calling me out on everything."

I shrugged. "With all that's happening, I guess I'm feeling a little insecure."

Matt chuckled. "You have nothing to be insecure about. I'm happy. Are you happy?"

I wrapped my arms around him and looked at the dark cherry cabinets and stainless steel appliances. "I can hardly wait to move here."

"Okay, close your eyes." Matt left the room and quickly returned with a bottle of champagne and wine glasses. "Let's have a toast to our new home."

Matt popped the cork on the bottle, and we drank. He touched my cheek and smiled. His sweet sexy smile demanded a smile in return, no matter how frustrated I was with him. Still, I couldn't help but wonder what it was that my instincts were warning me about.

CHAPTER 12

Momentarily disoriented, I awoke with my heart pounding. My eyes darted around the near empty bedroom. I realized where I was and dialed my anxiety down. "I had the worst nightmare."

Matt adjusted the pillows we had purchased the night before and slid his arm under my neck. "Tell papa."

"I went into a grocery store and you waited in the car. The checkout lines were long, and it took forever to get out of the store."

Matt chuckled. "You're right, that is a nightmare."

"I walked out to the car and saw you having sex with another woman."

"What?" Matt jerked his arm out from under me and got up. "Why would you tell me something like that? I told you I'm not seeing anyone."

Not the response I had expected. "Why are you mad? It was just a dream."

He stormed into the bathroom and slammed the door.

I figured morning sex was no longer an option, so wearing my cute new cropped pj set, I went downstairs to make coffee in the coffeemaker we had also purchased at Walmart, along with groceries for our first morning in the new house.

A short time later, Matt, wearing a t-shirt and boxer shorts, opened the French door and peered out at me watering plants in the backyard. "You have a text message from Steve. You want me to hand you your phone?" From the gentle tone of his voice, I surmised that the anger he'd expressed earlier had disappeared, but it hadn't.

"You screwing Steve? Is that why he's calling you here? Maybe you suspect me of cheating because you have a guilty conscience."

I put down the garden hose, rolled my eyes, and strolled back into the house. "I'm sorry my dream upset you."

"Yeah, me too." He stared out the kitchen window and exhaled a heavy sigh. "I overreacted upstairs and accused you of seeing Steve because I wanted to give you a taste of your own medicine." He poured himself a cup of coffee. "You want a refill on your coffee?"

"No, thanks." I read Steve's message: *Look how close we were to finding fifteen kilos of cocaine.*

"Everything okay?" Matt asked, admiring my scantily dressed body.

"Better than okay." Thrilled at seeing the attached picture, I recognized the cabinet in Rosa's garage. "I'm going back outside. I need to call Steve about work."

Matt kissed me on the head. "No need. I'm gonna go get dressed."

Eager to get details but lacking furniture, I hopped up on the kitchen counter and called Steve. "Let me guess, you somehow got a search warrant? You found the missing cocaine, and we're off the hook?"

"I'm going to put you on speaker because Paige is in the car with me," Steve said. "We're on our way back to the office."

I was surprised that Paige was back in town.

"And no, we didn't find it," Steve said. "But the lab guy said he found cocaine residue in that cabinet that I sent you a picture of. So, we're thinking that Londono sent one of his men to Rosa's to get it or the Colombians have it."

"Hopefully it's the Colombians," Paige added. "Because that means they will not be coming after the two of you."

"Were you able to arrest Rosa based on findings of residue?" I asked.

"Brace yourself," Steve said. "I know how much you two liked each other, so this is going to be tough for you to hear, but someone killed her."

Shocked, I now understood Paige's early return to Ft. Lauderdale, and what my gut instinct was warning me about. Rosa's death or disappearance was what I had subconsciously been worrying about. Nothing could happen to her. I needed her to retract her accusation. Now that would never happen.

It felt like all the oxygen had been sucked from the room.

"What about her mother and the kids?" I muttered.

"There was no sign of Rosa's mother or the two children," Paige said. "A lot of the children's clothes were missing and Rosa had her bag packed. I think she anticipated trouble and sent them someplace safe. The place was ransacked. They were definitely looking for money or the cocaine, and based on the torture they inflicted on Rosa, it looks like it was the cartel's handiwork." Paige paused. "Please tell me that you have a working security system at your new house, because if they don't have the drugs you and Steve will be their next targets."

"Why do you keep saying they?" I asked.

"The lab technician found two distinct sets of shoe prints at the Hernandez residence. But that is not important right now. What I am concerned about is the fact that with one simple online search of your married name, I found the address of your new home in Atlanta, and Londono can do the same."

"There's nothing I can do about that, Paige. Georgia doesn't have an exemption clause for law enforcement personnel regarding public records. Besides, Londono isn't gonna look for me anywhere except Florida. So, I'm not worried about it."

"Well, you should be," she replied. "Mullaney and Szish think if the people who killed Rosa don't have the drugs, they will continue their killing spree. Because of those concerns, Mullaney told Steve that both of you are getting police protection."

"I'm not happy about that," Steve shouted.

I chuckled at Steve's outburst. "Do you think it's possible that Londono had Rosa killed because he was afraid she was going to take us up on our offer for protection in exchange for information? Or that she was going to skip town with his drugs?"

"It looks like she was tortured for information she had," Paige replied. "Either the Colombians thought she knew where Londono stashed the missing cocaine, or Londono wanted to know what she did with it. If it were just a matter of her cooperating, they would have just flat-out killed her. Oh, and Mullaney wants you back here asap."

"Okay, I'll be back as soon as I can. I'll text you my flight information and would appreciate a ride from the airport."

I hung up, rushed upstairs, and found Matt straightening up our makeshift bed. "I have to get back to Florida. There's a new development in the case. Someone else has been murdered. Can you get me on the next flight out of here?"

Matt's eyebrows shot up and he made a call to his airline. Within an hour, he had me at the Atlanta airport. We walked briskly through the concourse, and Matt finally asked, "Was another cooperator killed?"

"No."

"Since we're back on this subject, what's being done to clear you of those allegations?"

"A polygraph."

"Okay, so once you take it, this will be over?"

I shrugged. "I don't know. I was hoping that this latest victim would eventually be charged with conspiracy to import and, in order to reduce her sentence, she would admit to lying about us taking the drugs. Now, that can't happen."

Matt furrowed his brow. "I thought that Londono character is the one who made the accusations. Who was killed?"

We stepped onto the airport escalator. I was silent until I was sure that no one could hear the conversation.

Matt impatiently glared at me. "You might as well tell me because I'm going to look it up on the Internet."

We got off the escalator and headed down a long, crowded corridor. "A woman named Rosa Hernandez. She was Londono's girlfriend."

Matt stopped dead in his tracks.

Stunned by his reaction, my heart raced. I stopped. "What? How do you know that name?"

He just stood there, frozen in place.

My words hung in the air. Panic set in. I swallowed hard. "Matt, talk to me. How do you know that woman?"

"She's a flight attendant," he finally stammered. "I worked with her."

I inhaled deeply and took his hand to continue on. "No, it's a common name. I assure you that this particular Rosa Hernandez was not a flight attendant."

Matt let out a sigh of relief. "You scared me. I thought I was going to discover that the woman was smuggling drugs into the United States on my flights from the Bahamas."

We continued down the corridor in search of my departure gate. "No, she has never been a flight attendant. Trust me on this."

Matt pointed to the line at gate number twenty. "Does Steve think the cartel killed her?"

"I don't know," I quietly replied, stepping in line. "Thank God her kids weren't at home."

Matt shook his head. "Women and children? I can't believe this. What kind of animals are you dealing with?"

"Drug traffickers," I calmly replied. "This is what they do."

Matt tilted his head in thought. "Doesn't it seem odd that you and Steve were targeted, but not Paige?"

Surprised by the question, I looked at him. "Uh, a little. Why do you ask?"

"Just seems odd," he said, watching passengers step into the jetway. "Remember to keep the alarm on at the house. I'll check with crew scheduling to see if I can I get a few days off or trade trips with someone."

I hugged him. "There's nothing you can do. So stay here and work. I'll be fine."

I knew that he would be safer on the job and in Atlanta than he would be at home. Putting on a brave face, I smiled at my concerned husband, and got on the plane.

Throughout the flight, I could not stop thinking. If the cartel didn't find the missing cocaine, Rosa's death is a sign of what is yet to come.

CHAPTER 13

An hour and a half later, I exited the Ft. Lauderdale airport. Paige was waiting in her government car curbside outside the terminal, just like we used to be able to do in the old days, pre-911.

I hopped in the car and she joined the flow of traffic, heading north. "Mullaney is waiting for us at his office."

I noticed Paige's serious demeanor, and thought about all the times I had joked with co-workers about me having a better sense of humor than Paige, but that wasn't true. Paige had a great sense of humor. She was just a little more selective about when she would display that side of her personality, and today was not that day.

On the ninth floor of the U.S. Attorney's Office, Paige signed the visitor's log and handed the pen to me. "I want to warn you that the crime-scene photos are very graphic."

Mullaney came out from behind a closed door and led us to a small conference room where Steve was already waiting. He dropped a manila folder on the table before pulling out a chair and sinking into it.

Paige eased into the chair next to Steve.

Tension filled the air.

The prosecutor's eyes settled on me. "I don't know how much Paige told you."

"Nothing," I replied, as my stomach tightened. I felt like a lamb being led to the slaughterhouse. The difference, the lamb doesn't know something bad is about to happen, and I did.

Mullaney pushed the folder over to me. I opened it and saw an array of horrific pictures from the Hernandez crime scene.

"She was mutilated and slowly bled to death," Mullaney explained. "The neighbor must have heard screams and decided to investigate." He pulled another picture out. It was of a body covered with so much blood that you couldn't tell if it was a man or a woman. "They found the neighbor on the ground between the two properties, also with her throat slit."

Having already viewed the crime scene firsthand, Paige only briefly looked at the pictures.

"At the residence, the drug dog hit on the washer, dryer, a cabinet in the garage, and the SUV, which had a hidden compartment in it," Mullaney said. "The lab confirmed that there was cocaine residue found in those locations. But no drugs or money were found."

Then, a photo caught my eye. A business card lying in a pool of Rosa's blood. It was my business card.

"Yep, they've got your number," Steve said.

Shivers ran down my spine.

Mullaney tapped on the table. "Save the jokes for the Improv." He glared at me. "It looks like someone was trying to tell police that you had something to do with this."

Steve shook his head. "Open your eye's. She's being set up."

"Or it's a message that Jenn is going to be the next victim," Paige retorted.

Outraged by Mullaney's comment, I fired back. "I've been in Atlanta since Friday. Check with the airline and the dozen or so people I had contact with. I left my card there the day Steve, and I paid her a visit. Maybe Londono found it and thought she was cooperating with us or maybe the message is like Paige said and they are coming after me next."

"I agree with Jennifer," Paige replied. "Why would you even imply that she had something to do with Rosa's murder? If anything, it looks like Londono is trying every way possible to discredit Jennifer. First saying that she ripped the load, and now her business card. This has to be retribution for his brother's death."

Ignoring Paige's comments, Mullaney shot Steve and me a peevish look. "If they got what they went there for, then it's over and the locals will follow up with the murder investigation. But if they didn't find the drugs because she moved the load, which one of our jailed cooperators confirmed is fifteen kilos, then a real danger still exists."

Mullaney's harsh eyes looked squarely at me and then at Steve. "Do either of you want police protection, because I can get it for you."

Both Steve and I declined, and no more was said about it. Mullaney, a former police officer with a concealed weapon permit, understood our ability to protect ourselves. "I thought you'd pass on that, but the local police will be driving by your homes on a regular basis and that is not open for further discussion."

"What about Londono?" Steve asked. "What did he have to say about Rosa's death?"

Mullaney looked away, out the window. "Nothing. We'll continue interviewing the people we have locked up. Mullaney pushed his chair away from the table. "Hopefully Londono will say something to a jailhouse snitch we have in the cell next to his. Other than that, it doesn't look like he's going to plead to anything. And both of you are scheduled for polygraph exams at nine o'clock tomorrow morning at the FBI."

After we retrieved our weapons and cell phones from the security lock boxes, Steve watched Paige make a call and took that opportunity to pull me aside. "You know that comment Mullaney made about your involvement in Rosa's death? Well, I think Mullaney is coming after you with everything he's got. He called me with questions about you threatening Rosa and why Londono would say we ripped him off."

"What did you tell him?"

"The truth," Steve replied. "I told him nothing was said that was not included in my report. I told him that I thought Londono framed us to discredit the government's case." Searching my eyes, Steve asked, "What else is there to tell?"

I looked over at Paige, who was putting her phone in her purse and unlocking her car. "Nothing."

After staring into my eyes for a long minute, Steve got into his car and drove off.

Paige and I drove in silence for a while until I said, "I need to ask you a favor."

Paige kept her eyes on the road. "Go ahead."

"I need you to run a trap and trace on calls to my phone, Matt's phone, and past calls to our home phone which we had disconnected."

Paige looked over at me and back at the cars in front of her. "Not until you tell me what is going on."

"I told you about the hang-up calls from a blocked number."

"You said that stopped."

"Yes, only to be replaced by cigarette butts in the yard."

"They could have blown in from the street."

I rolled my eyes. "Now, you sound like Matt."

"Why didn't you tell Mullaney?"

"Didn't see much point to it. He's not going to request a DNA test on those cigarette butts." I paused and chuckled. "Not unless you find my lifeless body near that type of evidence."

Paige gave me an appraising look. "Don't even joke about that."

"As for the calls, well, I think that will be a dead end." I shrugged. "But at this point, what have I got to lose? Seeing my card strategically placed in all that blood has convinced me that Londono is not finished with me. As if the story about us ripping the drugs wasn't enough. Now, he's trying to make it look like I'm involved in murder."

"Yeah, and how is he doing with that?" Paige sarcastically asked.

"A damn good job." I replied. "I only interacted with Rosa that one time." Frustrated, I shook my head. "What are we missing? He knows you're DEA. Yet, he didn't have Rosa say you ripped the drugs. Nor has he implicated you in any of this and you're the agent seated with Mullaney at the trial."

Paige shook her head in despair. "As I said, I think this is about the death of his brother."

I watched Paige biting her thumb nail, a habit I had not noticed before, and thought about what Matt had said about Paige not being targeted by Londono.

We entered my neighborhood. "I'll send a subpoena over to Mullaney first thing in the morning." Paige said as she pulled into my driveway. "But you need to call him tonight and tell him about the calls, the cigarettes, everything. Seeing a subpoena with your phone number on it without an explanation for the request will send him over the top. Assisting you, without his express blessing, will also cause my actions to be scrutinized. Something I can do without.

CHAPTER 14

IRS Supervisory Special Agent Rick Moore rested his elbow on his desk and pinched the bridge of his nose between his thumb and index finger. "Can she retake the polygraph?"

"I'll tell you what I told James Szish." Mullaney said, folding his arms across his chest. "I'm in trial. We need to keep moving forward on this case rather than spending valuable time trying to clear an agent who failed the exam." He glared over at me, seated in front of Moore's desk. "I'm going to be honest with you. Based on her responses to certain questions, I believe that I'm looking at our mole."

I recoiled. Anger welled up inside me and I remembered the question that made my heart rate accelerate. *"Have you ever provided any task force information to Eduardo Londono?"*

I thought back to the car ride when I told Londono how I was going to take him down based on what I knew about his money laundering operation with Rafael.

I cleared my tight throat. "Londono smugly suggested that he was going to walk on all charges. I merely corrected that assumption by pointing out the fact that Rafael's death locked in his grand jury testimony and maybe said a few other things pertaining to the strengths of my case."

Moore's brow arched. "Geez." He shifted his attention back to Mullaney. "Let her retake it. She'll write down exactly what was said and can be questioned about that."

"That doesn't explain the Orlando Perez leak," Mullaney said. "We've already done a sweep of the HIDTA offices and phones, and turned up nothing."

I rolled my eyes. "Oh please. There was no leak. I suggested we approach Orlando because he was the low hanging fruit. He was spending way more than he earned. Londono saw what Orlando was driving and how he was living and probably figured he was the next person we would attempt to flip. So, he got rid of him."

Mullaney glared at me. "Tell me about the money you received."

I shot a confused look at Mullaney, then Moore.

Moore lunged up from his chair. "Alright, this isn't an inquisition counselor. All you have is an inconclusive polygraph."

"No, there are unexplained expenditures," Mullaney replied, staring squarely at me. "Tell us about the twenty thousand dollars you used as a down payment for the new house you had built in Atlanta. The Treasury Inspector General's office traced it back to an out-of-state bank account in your mother's name. Those funds were newly deposited into your mother's account from some other bank, and we'll probably find another bank behind that." Grabbing his briefcase and walking to the door, Mullaney shot me a dirty look. "I plan on pursuing criminal charges. Get yourself a good attorney."

After Mullaney left, Moore shook his head and sat back down. "I'm on your side, but you know I have to report this to the SAC. He will most likely have me take your badge and weapon and place you on administrative leave. These are very serious charges. Reach out to your Federal Law Enforcement Officers representative and, like Mullaney suggested, get yourself a criminal attorney."

I got up, pulled the badge from my belt, and started to hand it to Moore.

He held up his hand. "You don't need to do that, at least not right now. Mullaney may have found you guilty, but all I see is an inconclusive polygraph. Let me talk to the SAC and we'll go from there." Moore paused. "What about the twenty thousand he referenced?

"It's a legitimate loan from my mother. Over the years, my mother deposited money into various banks to get a free gift or a better interest rate. To simplify things before she died, I closed those accounts and deposited that money into the account the twenty thousand came from."

Moore waved me out of his office. "Until this is resolved, find something else to work on. Talk to Julie. She could use some help with the brokerage statements in her securities fraud case."

The IRS office was completely empty, much like I felt. I flopped into the chair at my desk. The Treasury Inspector General would find me clear of any wrong doing, but in the meantime I would be suspended. Even if I got out from under this, no attorney or agent would ever want to work with me. They would always wonder about me. The rumor mill among agents ran more rampant than gossip between teenage girls.

It was official. The bottom had dropped out of my life. Londono was going to accomplish exactly what he had set out to do, create doubt in the minds of the jurors, while at the same time ruining my career. I reflected back on Paige's words the day of Londono's arrest. "You're playing with fire." She was right. I should have never taunted the beast. Now, Londono not only wanted an acquittal, but revenge for having his younger brother imprisoned where he died.

This case had me by the throat. Now, it was my turn to suffer.

My desk phone rang. I answered it and heard a friendly voice. "Jennifer, this is Robin in Atlanta. It's probably nothing, but after hearing about the kind of work you do, and knowing that your house is empty, I jotted down the license plate number of a car I saw parked in your driveway on a couple of evenings."

I scribbled the Florida tag number on my desk calendar and did a ChoicePoint database search. It appeared that Paige was correct again. Londono had discovered the new home. But how would he have known about the Georgia house, unless someone had told him? The question was who.

I heard the shuffling of papers, got up, and peered into Julie Owens' cubicle. "Where is everyone?"

Julie, a confident auburn-haired woman, with the body of a fitness trainer, motioned at the clock on the wall. "At home or at happy hour. It's five thirty on a federal Friday."

"What are you still doing here?" I asked.

"Waiting for you. I heard some loud voices behind closed doors. You want to talk now or after you've had a few drinks at Laurel's party?"

"Shit. With everything that's been going on, I forgot about the Christmas party. I promised Laurel that I would make her favorite appetizer. I have some cooking to do. Let's chat later."

I quickly threw the files that were on my desk into a briefcase and scrambled out of the office. My career was circling the drain, and I wanted to prevent the same from happening with my personal life.

I surprised myself by remembering that I needed more olive oil and another jar of spaghetti sauce to make my appetizers, and pulled into the plaza near my house on the way home. The nail salon next to the grocery store had windows decorated in red and gold for the holidays. The toy store at the end of the plaza advertised a photo opportunity with Santa. I watched women bustling around in their busy lives. They were thinking about work, their families, and getting their Christmas shopping done. Days earlier, that was me. My biggest and most urgent personal concern was finding a box large enough to hold the model plane I had purchased for Matt and had hidden at Laurel's house.

Now, my life was a train wreck. I was being accused of being in league with the devil and getting two of my informants killed, and, if that wasn't bad enough, I probably had a Colombian cartel wanting to kill me right after they tortured me for information that I didn't have. All the shock, fear, and dread that had originally gripped me was dissipating. My new focus had to be that of proving my innocence.

I opened the driver's side door of my car and a hand grabbed my arm. I whipped around to defend myself, and was staring into Paige's boyfriend's face.

"I didn't mean to frighten you," Ron said.

I stared at his shaved head and salt and pepper beard. A new look since I had seen him months earlier. "No, I'm fine. How are you?"

"Concerned about Paige. I dropped off some groceries at her house that week she said she would be in Fort Myers. The nanny is able to track Paige's location via her cell phone. The kids like to see where their mother is. So she does it for them."

I nodded and shrugged.

"I was there when the kids asked the nanny to do that, and it showed Paige's phone in Miami, not Fort Myers. I asked Paige about it and she said she had to keep driving back and forth for the case, but that didn't make sense. When I spotted you, I thought I'd see what you knew about it. Should I be concerned?"

"Like you, I thought she was in Fort Myers. Although, she did have to come back here unexpectedly due to a development in our case. The nanny probably activated the mobile phone tracker around the time Paige had just gotten back into town."

He looked down at the ground, nodded in agreement, and finally said, "Well, if I don't see you before Christmas, have a great holiday."

"Thank you. And you as well." I watched Ron walk away and wondered why Paige was being so secretive about where she was and what she was doing."

I also wondered about my phone and if some cell phone tracking application was how Londono found my

Newnan home. I would have to discuss that with our tech agents.

It was six o'clock when I arrived home. I couldn't stop mentally kicking myself for everything that had transpired. I should have kept my emotions in check and never have threatened to destroy Londono. Who could have known that my stupid actions would have set off such a nightmarish chain of events?

While pacing my kitchen, I frantically called Steve and got his voice mail. After leaving a message, I opened the refrigerator, in dire need of a glass of wine. There, lining the shelves, were the ingredients I had purchased to make appetizers for Laurel and Richard's annual Christmas party. After everything that had happened, I was not in the mood to cook or socialize, but I had promised Laurel that I would prepare my spicy Italian meatballs and didn't want to let her down.

Worried about me, Matt had swapped trips with another pilot and had arrived home the previous day. It was comforting to have him home on days like the one I just had. So as not to put a damper on the evening, I had decided not to tell him about Mullaney's threat of criminal prosecution until after Laurel's party.

Sweaty from mowing the yard, Matt walked into the kitchen, grabbed a bottle of water from the pantry, and chugged it. With the scent of garlic, basil, and tomato sauce wafting through the house, he grabbed a fork and speared a small meatball from the sauce in the slow cooker.

"Have you given the Atlanta address to any of your pilot friends, so they could go check it out?" I asked. "Maybe gauge the driving distance to the airport if they were to bring their car to Atlanta."

"No, but I do have a few guys who said they'd stop by to check it out next week when I'm there. Why?"

"Do you know a woman by the name of Olivia Ogden, or a pilot with that last name?" I asked Matt, as he blew on the hot meatball, then devoured it.

"Don't think so. Why?"

I turned the slow cooker on the high setting. "Robin saw a car with Florida plates at our Atlanta house. The car came back to an Olivia Ogden. If you don't know that name, or this person wasn't there for rental purposes, then it was most likely one of Londono's men."

Matt abruptly stopped chewing the food in his mouth and threw his fork across the kitchen with such intensity that it left an indentation on the wall. "God damn it. What's wrong with you?" He bellowed. "You're obsessed with this shit. And now you've got Robin involved?" He pursed his lips. "First, it was hang-up calls and now cars in our driveway. In case you forgot your geography, Georgia is the state above Florida, so there are probably a lot of cars with Florida license plates in that area. I can't take any more of this." He grabbed his car keys and stormed out of the house.

Surprised by his reaction, I decided to save the failed polygraph story for another night.

CHAPTER 15

Promptly at seven o'clock, Paige arrived at my front door carrying a decorative gift basket and a plate of cookies. "I think the local police just did their early evening drive-by of your house."

With a tray of meatballs in hand, I pulled the front door shut behind me and scanned the street. "Yeah, they pass by every few hours."

We entered Laurel's foyer, amazed at how many people were in attendance for the party. "There's gotta be fifty people here," Paige shouted over the cacophony of voices and music.

Making our way past a decorative tiered buffet table covered with appetizers, I leaned in toward Paige so as not to yell. "Let's find our hostess."

Paige dropped her gift basket under the brightly lit Christmas tree and grabbed each of us a glass of champagne as we strolled past the bar. "She sure went all out on food and alcohol for this event."

We found Laurel and another friend, Anne, in the kitchen, making some concoction in the blender. Because of everything that had been happening, I had not seen or spoken to either of them in weeks. Anne brushed a wisp of her silky brown hair from her olive skin and gave me a peck on the cheek. "Long time no see."

I nodded and helped her clear a place on the counter for the meatballs and cookies.

Laurel, a petite blonde with a contagious smile, greeted us enthusiastically. "Happy holidays." And shoved a drink in my hand. "Tell me how this mojito tastes?"

Not wanting to explain that I disliked mint, I took a small sip of the drink in the fancy plastic glass and nodded. "It's perfect and I taste fresh mint."

"That's the exact response I had hoped for." A slightly tipsy Laurel giggled and rushed off with her tray of fresh mojitos.

To avoid the crowd at the inside bar and find a place where we could hear each other speak, Paige and I wandered out to the patio where there was another fully stocked bar next to yet another long festooned buffet table loaded with food. On the way out of the house, I spotted two other close female friends that I had again not spent any time with since Londono's arrest, Karen and Kim.

Paige and I waved at them from across the room, and made our way outside, where Paige helped herself to various cheese and cracker snacks while I went for the peel and eat shrimp.

We grabbed an empty high-top table overlooking the brightly lit fountain situated out in the middle of the lake, and began eating.

After a long drink of champagne, Paige said, "As you requested, we did a quick analysis of your phone records. Unfortunately, none of the incoming calls could be traced back to any known devices belonging to Londono or his people."

"Burner phones," I commented. "Is there any way to determine who purchased the phone that the calls had originated from?"

"Nope, waste of time. They would have been purchased with cash, so there would be no record of who owns the phone." Paige took a bite of cheese and wiped her mouth with her napkin. "I did one other thing. I picked a random sample of calls, starting with the date of Londono's arrest through last week, and checked to see which cell towers they were hitting. I found that some of the earlier calls had pinged off a tower near Rosa's house."

"Londono must have instructed one of his men, guarding the drugs at her location, to call Matt and our house to spook me."

Paige nodded. "The more recent calls were most likely telemarketers because they hit on a tower in Ft. Lauderdale and in a place called Newnan, Georgia."

I almost choked on my food. "Holy shit. That's where my house is."

Paige looked up from her plate, her mouth agape.

"I tell people our house is in Atlanta because no one has ever heard of Newnan. But that means that it was Londono's people at my house in Georgia."

Paige set her drink down. "What?"

"Our realtor saw a car at the house, and when I ran the tag, it came back to some woman in Ft. Lauderdale. I need to tell Mullaney."

"I wouldn't," Paige said, plucking a shrimp from my plate. "I shared my phone findings with him. He said the calls were not enough to prove that Londono was harassing you. Instead, he plans to turn those calls against you and introduce them as evidence of communication between you and Londono."

My stomach dropped. Once again, Londono was one step ahead of me. "Of course, Londono wasn't trying to get under my skin. He was setting me up."

Paige nodded in agreement. "Makes sense. Another thing I was thinking about is if Londono had his people watching Rosa's place. They must have seen her mother and kids leave. That makes me think that Londono did have her killed because he suspected that she was going to take the drugs and run."

"But why torture her?"

Paige pondered the question while finishing her drink. "Because she moved the drugs, and he wanted to know where or he wanted it to look like the Colombians did it."

I finished the last gulp of my champagne. "Mullaney has it out for me because I failed my polygraph. I take it that you passed with flying colors."

"Haven't taken it yet."

That seemed strange, but I continued on. "Actually, mine was inconclusive, but he thinks I'm the person feeding information to Londono, and he threatened me with criminal prosecution. Mullaney must not have scheduled you because he thinks he's found the leak, me."

"Shit, you should have told me. I would have bottom drawered the phone records for a few weeks. Now, that information may have sealed your fate."

Distraught, I covered my face with my hands. "I don't know what to do."

In an attempt to console me, Paige reached across the table and touched my hand. "It's all circumstantial. I know this is all Londono and we'll prove it."

I sighed, releasing a lung full of tension. "Work, my marriage, it's all falling apart. Matt's had it with me. I can't say anything without him getting mad."

Paige shrugged. "Well, can you blame him? You wouldn't be happy with him if the situation were reversed."

"No matter what I say, he either dismisses it or tells me I'm being paranoid. My life used to be so wonderful and lately nothing makes sense. Our relationship is really strained." I looked out at the lake and took a deep breath. "Okay, enough about me. How are you and Ron? And why isn't he here with you?"

"We're fine. He wouldn't know anyone here, so I thought it better to come alone."

"Sure." I paused and thought about my earlier encounter with her boyfriend. "Since Londono's arrest, it seems like all we ever talk about is my problems. You know I'm here if you ever want to talk about what's going on in your life."

Paige gazed over my shoulder. "Speak of the devil, Matt's here."

I sat up straight and wiped the tears from my cheeks.

"How are you doing?" Matt asked Paige.

"Great," Paige replied. "Ron and I are thinking about having a New Year's Eve party. Can we count on the two of you to attend?"

Taking a long slow drink from his bottle of beer, Matt apprehensively said, "Uh, that sounds fun, but unfortunately I'm working."

Paige scowled. "Okay, Ron can take me out to an expensive dinner." She held up her empty glass. "Jenn, Matt, another?"

I handed Paige my empty glass. "I think I'll switch to white wine."

Matt held up a nearly full bottle of beer. "I'm good."

Paige nodded and left.

Not looking up from my plate, I dipped a shrimp in cocktail sauce. "Really? You're working New Year's Eve?"

That was all it took to set Matt off again. In a low angry voice, he growled, "Oh, don't start this here and now." And he stormed off.

Witnessing Matt's dramatic departure, Paige returned to the table accompanied by Julie, who raised her glass in a toast. "Well done, Jenn."

I shrugged. "Yep, being paranoid and pissing my husband off seems to come naturally these days. I better go see if I can talk him down."

I walked next door to our house and found Matt in our living room watching television. "What's going on?"

"I'm tired of you complaining about my schedule."

I nodded that I understood. "You're flying out in the morning, so I don't want to fight. Maybe we need to move the timeframe up on our relocation to Atlanta so we won't be spending so many weekends and holidays apart."

He stared blankly at the television. "I'm also fed up with your paranoid suspicions. Every phone call and every car that drives down our street is a drug dealer. When a cigarette blows into our yard, it's a potential bomb."

I couldn't believe his exaggerations. He had obviously been holding all this pent up anger inside.

Defending my actions only further fueled Matt's fire. He jumped up from the sofa, walked briskly to the bedroom and, before slamming the door, yelled, "Don't tell me you're being cautious! You're obsessed and paranoid! Frankly, Jenn, I'm tired of it!"

Hurt and mad, I stormed out of the house and back to the party. I needed another drink.

"Leave it alone," Paige said. "All this probably scares him or makes him feel helpless. Men don't like to have those feelings."

"You have a good marriage," Julie added. "Don't let this case destroy it."

I thanked my friends for their support and hung out with them until late into the night. Matt never came back to the party.

It was close to two in the morning before I went home. Before going to bed, I performed my nightly ritual of methodically walking through the house, turning off lights and locking doors.

On the foyer table, I noticed that the picture of me and Matt was lying face down. Setting it upright, a broken piece of glass fell from the frame. *Did Matt do this in a fit of rage, or did it just fall over by accident?*

I jarred the table to test my theory that it was a mishap. Nothing happened. The picture did not move. Matt or someone broke the picture on purpose. *Stop it*, I told myself. Stop making something out of nothing. It was an old, cheap frame. Maybe the glass had been cracked for a while.

I started to walk away, and that's when I heard a noise. It was outside the front door, a shuffling sound. I didn't see anyone through the peephole. Gingerly, I turned the door handle and pushed hard against the door.

"AAAAIIIIEEEE," Laurel screamed and popped out from behind the door. "Oh my god, you scared me. I didn't see any lights on, so I thought you had gone to bed." Laurel held up a piece of paper. "I came over to remove the note I left for your friends that said the party was next door."

"I'm so sorry," I chuckled.

Laurel giggled. "See you tomorrow."

I rubbed my aching head and realized that Matt was right about my paranoia. Then, glancing down, guilt turned to fear. The same cigarette butts that I had found at the mailbox were now right outside my door. They couldn't have blown from the street up into our alcove. Did someone watching my house see the opportunity to come searching for the drugs I had been accused of taking? And worse yet, did the intruder encounter Matt.

Once again, dread twisted in my gut. Matt had not returned to the party, and that was not like him. What if they took him in hopes of making me talk? Panicking, I raced back to the bedroom. Visions of the two slain women ran through my mind. I threw the bedroom door open. My body shook with fear. It was dark. The blackout curtains were closed. The light from the living room barely illuminated the room. I moved closer to the bed. "Matt?" My heart was pounding out of my chest. I pulled back the comforter. Matt rolled over and repositioned his body on the bed. I exhaled loudly. *I don't know how much more I can take.*

CHAPTER 16

The next morning, I awoke to an empty bed. It was the first time Matt had left without saying goodbye. A tear rolled onto my pillow. My life was so messed up. I stared at the ceiling. Matt was my everything. I remembered our first kiss, and the first time we made love. I wiped the tears away. "It's all my fault. I'm driving him away. I'll do better and watch what I say to him."

Our nightly phone calls were brief and about nothing in particular. Neither of us mentioned the fight.

A few days later, Matt returned from his trip. Things between us seemed to be fine, especially when he heard that I was off the Londono case. Due to the tension in the marriage, I didn't tell him about Mullaney's most recent unfounded accusations.

New Year's Eve morning, I suggested that I fly with Matt so we could bring the new year in together.

He smiled and stroked my face. "That wouldn't be any fun for you. I have three legs and I end late in some city in the Carolinas." Kissing me passionately, he ran his hand between my legs. "I have a better idea."

He knew exactly where and how to touch me. When he had me on the brink of orgasm, he rolled on top of me, slid my arms above my head, and entered me. His intensity and hardness made my breath catch. I grabbed his face, and we devoured each other, moving in rhythm until the passion exploded.

Afterwards, he blanketed my body for a minute before tenderly kissing me and rolling onto his side of the bed.

I hiked myself up on an elbow and admired his toned body. "I love you."

Matt lovingly gazed at me and gently swept a stray hair from my cheek. "I love you too."

Feeling satisfied, loved and cherished, I put on my white silk robe and strolled to the shower. The warm water cascaded over my body. Once again, all was well in the world. I had so much love for my husband. I couldn't imagine my life without him. He was my lover, and my best friend. If only I could clear myself of those ridiculous allegations. I stepped out of the shower, wiped off the steamed up mirror, and glared at my image. "Come on girl. Think positive. You've done nothing wrong, so the only thing to come from all of this is idle gossip. In a few months you can start anew in Atlanta."

Matt tapped on the bathroom door. "You almost finished in there?"

Happy for the interruption, I slipped back into my robe. "It's all yours."

There was a sly look on Matt's face. Maybe he had switched flights with another pilot so he could be home with me. He took my hand and led me into the kitchen, where I found a fresh bouquet of flowers, a DVD, and a note. *Happy New Year! Look in the fridge.*

In the refrigerator was a bottle of champagne and my all-time favorite food, King crab legs. I wrapped my arms around Matt's neck. "Thank you. You're such a wonderful husband."

Matt chuckled and handed me a cup of coffee. "Since you're staying in tonight, I just wanted you to have a nice New Year's Eve."

"Actually, I'm spending the night at Julie's. So, thank you for the lovely contributions to our little New Year's Eve party."

Matt slid an egg onto a plate, along with toast, and passed it to me. "Great, I'm happy that you have plans. Now if you'll excuse me, I have to shower and hit the road." With a cup of coffee in hand, Matt strolled out of the kitchen.

I grabbed a handful of bills off my desk and began going through them over breakfast.

A half hour later, Matt reappeared, clean shaven, and in uniform. He gently kissed me. "Okay, I'm out of here." Just the sight of him caused my body to ache for him again. My insides tightened, and I pulled him closer.

He chuckled. "Jenn, I can't miss this flight up to Atlanta. I'll call you later."

I admired his physique as I watched him fill his travel mug with coffee. "Matt?" He glanced over at me. "What's up?"

"When you return home, can we take some time to talk about our relationship? I love you and I don't want to lose you."

Matt offered his irresistible smile. "Yep, we'll get through this."

Not wanting to push the issue any further, I changed the subject. "Also, when you have a chance, can you contact your cell phone carrier about a couple of items?"

He secured the lid on his travel mug. "Yeah sure, what's wrong?"

I stared down at an invoice. "Well, it looks like the changes you made to your service resulted in a $167.00 cell phone bill. Under the other contract, I thought you were only paying $50.00 a month."

"I was." He looked over my shoulder at the bill. "Something's not right. Also, I signed up for paperless billing." He shrugged. "I'll straighten it out when I get home." He gave me a peck on the cheek and was out the door.

It made me sad to watch him leave. It was a lot easier being the one leaving versus the spouse being left behind. And this was especially true for the holidays. Unfortunately, it would have been impossible for me to get a seat on any of his overbooked flights or enjoy our new home in Atlanta that had just been rented out to some of Matt's pilot friends. The only thing left was relaxation at home, which was not such a bad alternative since the hang-up calls had stopped. Still, I couldn't shake an eerie feeling I had and wondered if this was just the calm before the storm.

Late afternoon Julie called and cancelled our New Year's Eve plans. Her daughter was sick. Disappointed, and with the sun setting on the horizon, there was only one thing to do, go jogging. I needed to figure out Londono's next move, and running would be the perfect way to do that.

Dressed in shorts and a T-shirt, I pounded the sidewalk at a brisk pace. Think, I told myself. What more could Londono do, short of having me killed? I scoffed out a breath. If that was his plan, he would have already done it. No, his best strategy would be to move on to Paige, or Mullaney, and discredit them. The evening sky grew dark. I turned around and headed back to the house. I didn't want that to happen to Paige. She was my closest friend and had stood by me despite all the false allegations.

I scanned my surroundings as street lights flickered on in my quiet residential neighborhood. Nothing was out of the ordinary. Still, I wondered if Londono's men could be watching. My phone vibrated. I flinched.

"I'm grabbing a bite to eat and then flying to Nashville," Matt said. "How did the crab claws turn out?"

"Haven't gotten to them," I said, short of breath. "I'm out jogging."

"Yeah, it sounds like it," Matt replied. "I have a pretty tight schedule and there are delays, so this will probably be the only chance I'll have to wish you a happy new year."

I slowed my pace to a walk up to the front of our house. "I wish you were here."

"Me too. I'll call you tomorrow."

I entered the house and noticed how empty it was without Matt.

After a shower, and a few glasses of champagne, I curled up on the sofa and found myself lost in the movie, *Unfaithful*.

The tension grew as the husband became ever more suspicious that his wife was having an affair. He wanted to see the other man and convince him to end the relationship.

Surely the man had pursued his wife; what other explanation could there be? His wife would never do anything to disrupt their wonderful life. At least that is what he thought until he saw the snow globe he had given his wife for their one-year wedding anniversary. There it was, sitting on a shelf at the other man's apartment. In that instant, the Richard Gere character realized his wife had given away a special gift that was a token of his love.

Manic disturbing music played in the background as Gere, blinded by rage, smashed the heavy glass globe into the man's scull BAM!

I jumped, not because of what was unfolding on the screen, but because of the loud sound at my house. The glass patio door shook. I gasped. It was impossible to see who was outside because of the reflection of the living room light on the door. I lunged behind the loveseat and yanked the light cord from the wall socket. Crouched low to the floor, I turned to race into the bedroom to retrieve my weapon when I heard Laurel shout, "Jenn, it's me."

I peered out from behind the love seat.

She knocked on the door again, and called out, "Happy New Year."

I stood up and grabbed up the remote to mute the movie on my way to the door.

Laurel stood there laughing.

I opened the door.

"I didn't mean to startle you, but you should have seen yourself. I saw lights and thought I should investigate. Did your plans with Julie fall through?"

I pointed to a bowl of crab shells and a half-empty bottle of champagne on the table. "Yes, her daughter has the flu. So, here I sit. What are you doing home? I thought you had to work."

Laurel handed me a plate of stuffed shrimp. "We had enough people working at the restaurant, so we cut out early to watch the fireworks here on the patio. Come join us."

Laurel was such a thoughtful friend. Knowing how often Matt was out of town, she always included me in her family activities.

"Come on, we have ten minutes until midnight," she coaxed.

"Okay." I put the plate of shrimp in the refrigerator and followed Laurel to her patio, where her husband, Richard, was setting up chairs.

A slight chill filled the air, but nothing that warranted anything more than a sweater. The professional fireworks display above the park was a magnificent and colorful show, but short lived.

"Happy New Year," I gleefully shouted into my phone, leaving Matt a voice mail message. "You're missing a great party. We have fireworks, food, lots of wine, and I'm getting to know some of the people from around the lake." Slurring my words slightly, I added, "Wish you were here."

By one o'clock, the activity was scaling down. Feeling the effect of all the alcohol, I stumbled through my house, turning off lights and double checking door locks before plopping into bed. I chugged a full glass of water along with three Advil. Instead of counting sheep, I was counting drinks. *Let's see. Before Laurel came over, I consumed half a bottle of champagne. For the next hour, I had wine, more champagne and jello shots. Yep, I'm gonna have a hangover,* I thought as I drifted off to sleep.

***

I was startled awake by the loud shrieking sound of our security alarm. I jumped out of bed and grabbed my 9mm Sig Sauer from the nightstand. I cautiously opened the bedroom door to see if there was any movement in the house. Not seeing anyone, I sprinted to the foyer, where I turned on a light and punched in a code on the alarm panel. That killed the loud piercing noise.

Then my cell phone rang. With the sound of my heart pounding in my ears, I ran back to the bedroom and grabbed up the phone. "Hello, yes, I'm the homeowner and I just turned the alarm off. Can you stay on the phone with me while I walk through my house?" With weapon in hand, I cleared the rest of the house and responded to the man on the phone. "As far as I can tell, it was a false alarm. Maybe some thunder or fireworks set it off."

"Yes, we've had a lot of that tonight," the man informed me.

I ended the call and decided to once again check all the doors and windows before going back to bed. "What the hell?" I hissed. The front door deadbolt was not in the locked position. My blood pressure spiked. With my gun in my right hand, I grabbed the door knob with my left hand, and pushed the door open. No one was there.

I locked up and said aloud, "I'm losing my mind."

CHAPTER 17

Two nights later, Matt returned home. I told him what had happened, and once again, it turned into a fight.

I stormed away from Matt and into the bedroom to change into my workout clothes. "You're not going to talk me out of this. I have to tell Mullaney and my supervisor that we had an attempted break-in."

Matt followed me, raking his hands through his hair. "I'm not trying to talk you out of anything. I just hate to see you make a fool of yourself because I'm not so sure you locked the door to begin with. You know it doesn't latch properly unless you hold it shut and push on it when you turn the deadbolt, and from that voice message you left me, you sounded pretty drunk."

"Why are you not believing me? I know that I locked the door." I shouted. "With everything that has been happening, I constantly make sure our doors are locked." Disgusted with Matt's unsympathetic reaction, I picked up my phone. "I'll check with the police. Maybe they saw something."

Matt scoffed. "You think the police are going to provide you with information about suspicious vehicles in our neighborhood?"

"Sure, why not? They've been doing drive-bys of ......" My words drifted off when I saw a dark expression cross Matt's face.

His eyebrows arched. "What? Now, you've got the police watching our house?"

I took a deep breath and put my phone down. I had forgotten that I hadn't told him about my business card being found in Rosa's blood or me failing the polygraph, and about how Mullaney had arranged for the locals to conduct drive-bys.

"When were you going to tell me this?"

I swallowed past the tightening in my throat. "When you're not angry." Then, in a solemn tone added, "Which seems like never, lately."

"Of course I'm angry." Matt shrugged off his jacket and threw it on the bed. "You scrutinize my phone calls. You have your agent friends spying on me."

My hands rose to my hips. "Who's do I have spying on you?"

"Joel."

"Oh, that was a fluke."

Matt rubbed his forehead. "When is this going to be over? When are you going to stop sending the neighbor's cigarette butts out to be analyzed, or running the tags on every car that drives past our homes?"

I shook my head at his exaggeration. A tense silence stretched between us.

"You're overreacting," Matt spat. "I'm not saying that the alarm didn't go off. I just think there are other, more realistic, things that could have caused it, such as fireworks."

A knot of anger formed in my chest. Matt's reluctance to believe anything I said caused me to explode. "For once, take my side and stop telling me that I'm crazy or wrong! If you can't do that, then go stay at your parents' condo."

Time stopped. We both stood there glaring at each other. I wondered if Matt would grab some clothes and leave. What happened next should have deescalated the situation, but for me it set off loud alarm bells. Matt's phone rang, and he ignored it. Now, most men would take the call, any call, as a distraction. It's the perfect excuse to walk away from a fight with your spouse.

Not Matt. He gathered up his jacket and hung it in the closet. Even after his phone rang a second time, he ignored it.

Next time it rings, I'll just grab it from him. I won't say a word and I'll see who is on the other end.

94

Unfortunately, before I could execute my plan, Matt turned the phone to vibrate and shoved it in his pocket. "Why aren't you answering that?" I asked, with venom in my voice.

"Because it's Gary," Matt replied in an agitated tone. "I'll call him later."

With my hand out, I distrustfully asked, "Can I see?"

Matt shot me a dirty look and reluctantly handed me his phone. I scrolled through his most recent calls and saw Gary's name numerous times.

Ashamed, I dialed down my anger. "I'm sorry."

Before storming from the room, he yelled out, "Here are the facts. You were drunk. There is no sign of a break-in, and as far as my phone is concerned, if I get any strange calls, I'll turn it over to the government so you can conduct a thorough investigation, Agent Weber."

I needed to clear my mind and work off all my pent up anger. I grabbed my gym bag and headed toward Bally's Fitness as I did most evenings after work on the nights Matt was out of town.

***

More than a workout, I needed to talk with an ally. Parked in Paige's driveway, I pushed a button on my phone and stared at the upper middle-class house, in a pristine Coconut Creek neighborhood filled with two-story beige, salmon, and cream colored homes.

Paige answered on the second ring. "Are you parked in front of my house?"

"Yep, Matt and I had a fight. Can I come in?"

The front door opened. Paige stood in the doorway and watched her two adorable children run to greet me. "Can you have dinner with us?" Hannah asked.

95

"We're having spaghetti," Mark proudly announced, taking my hand and pulling me up toward the door.

Inside, Paige held up a bottle of red wine. "Want a drink?"

"I've been drinking way too much lately," I said, taking a seat at the kitchen counter. "But yes, I need a drink

The two children enthusiastically chatted to me about school and dinner until Paige distracted them. "You guys can watch television for a half hour, while I talk with Jennifer and finish cooking."

The pair gleefully ran into the next room and argued over the program they wanted to watch. Paige shook her head and poured two glasses of wine.

I drank half the glass and poured more. "Matt is not the supportive husband he used to be, and I don't know what to do to repair our relationship."

"Maybe you need a break from each other and the craziness. You're not tied down on a case, so why not get away for a while. Go visit your friends in Tampa or Los Angeles. Londono or the cartel won't track you there."

I pondered the idea as I sipped my wine. "I'd be worried about Matt. If they can't get to me, they may do something to him." I paused. "I think Londono's men tried to break into my house New Year's Eve."

Paige stopped chopping lettuce and glared at me. "While you were at Julie's?"

"Nope, I was home, asleep. The alarm went off around two in the morning. I didn't see anyone. When they jiggled the door, the alarm must have scared them off."

Paige tossed cherry tomatoes over the lettuce she had placed in a large wooden bowl. "You need surveillance cameras."

"Yes," I said, snagging a tomato from the cutting board. "Because Londono doesn't know that I'm no longer on the case, I think he sent someone to hide cocaine in my house, tip off police, and get me arrested and removed from the case." I paused and raised a brow. "Or maybe he's finally tired of toying with me and wanted me dead."

Paige stopped what she was doing, and in a sharp tone, said, "Dead or in jail. I knew that you verbally sparing with him in the car was going to come back and bite you in the ass."

Her words caused a chill to run down my spine, and got me to think about what was really happening. "You're right. As a law enforcement agent locked behind bars, I would undoubtedly be killed by another prisoner. That's it. He wants me to die in jail like his brother did."

CHAPTER 18

The next morning, I sat at the table staring into a cup of coffee. "I'm not in the mood for the range today." Matt slid a plate of toast in front of me. "I'm sorry about our fight."

"So many arguments lately. We never used to fight," I said, admiring how handsome Matt looked in his uniform. "When will you be back?"

"This is only a two-day trip. So I'll be home tomorrow evening." He placed a hand on my shoulder in an attempt to get me to look at him. "We haven't been out on a Saturday night in a long time. How about tomorrow night? We can stay out late, drink and talk. The best part is that you can sleep in and recuperate all day Sunday."

He kissed me on the cheek, and before exiting the kitchen, added, "Hell, to sweeten the pot, I'll even throw in Sunday morning brunch down at the beach."

"Sounds nice." I walked him out to his car. "I also keep forgetting to ask you about your cell phone bill. Did you call about that?"

"Yep, it was a billing mistake." He tossed his travel bag and flight case into the trunk of the car. "They're going to credit my account." He kissed me again, jumped into the car, and left.

As I watched him drive away, I had an uneasy feeling. Something about this trip bothered me. Was it because I felt things had not been settled between us? Or was this some bizarre premonition or forewarning that something bad was going to happen, possibly to Matt's plane?

Whatever the weird sensation was, I tried to shake it off, but it would not go away. Nothing like that had ever happened to me before. I ran into the house and grabbed my phone.

Matt needed to be careful or pay particular attention to anything out of the norm. His phone rang numerous times and went to voice mail. He probably had the car radio blasting and didn't hear it.

I thought about it and quickly ended the call. Anything I would say would further reinforce Matt's belief that I was paranoid, maybe to the point of needing therapy. Why create more tension between us?

I wandered into the bedroom closet, grabbed ear protection and extra magazines for my weapon, and tossed them into a duffel bag for my quarterly weapons qualification.

On the drive down to the shooting range in Plantation, I received a call from an unknown number. I eased the phone to my ear, thinking it would be a taunting threat from one of Londono's men. Instead, the male on the phone identified himself as Parkland Police Officer Timothy Carr. "I am one of the officers that was on duty in the early morning hours of January 1," he said. "You told the desk officer that your alarm went off at approximately 2:00 a.m. My notes indicate that we were patrolling the Regency Lakes development at that time. We exited your development around 1:30, and prior to our departure, we did not note any suspicious activity."

"Thank you for the call, Officer Carr." What was I thinking? I should have known that the person who attempted to break into my house had been watching the place and the timing of police patrols.

I pulled my car into a parking space and glared out at the paper targets that had been hung down range. I took my place in the hot morning sun at the twenty-five yard line and realized the feeling I had experienced earlier had nothing to do with instinct or intuition. I was getting sick. It started with a headache and soon evolved into a sore throat. I toughed it out for the next few hours, knowing it was more of a hassle to reschedule a range date than it was to just go and be done with it until the next quarter.

My head pounded with each round of loud gunfire and the rancid smoke burned my throat.

At the 15-yard line, I was waiting for the targets to turn when the instructor walked up behind me and commented about the loose grouping of shots on my target. "Jennifer, this is not like you. Concentrate."

When the targets faced again, I took two shots that landed an inch apart in the groin area of the human silhouette target and glanced over my shoulder at the on-looking instructor. He threw his hands up into the air and mouthed the words "point taken."

By noon, stress and exertion had finally taken its physical toll on me. The rundown feeling I had woken up with had quickly escalated. Rather than going out to lunch with my co-workers after the qualification, I went home. I called in sick and jumped into a hot shower. I needed to rinse the gunpowder from my hair and skin, and wash two cold tablets down with a tall glass of ice water. Weezer, my black cat, lay fast asleep on the sofa, and it occurred to me that I should do the same.

Early evening the sky grew dark and a wind from the west created white caps on the usually calm lake. I turned the television on and curled up on the sofa to channel surf. Matt often poked fun at me for liking what he called chic flicks. But since he wasn't home, that was exactly what I was going to do. Soon the rain pummeled the barrel tile roof of our house with such intensity that Weezer decided to hide under my blanket.

I settled on a Lifetime Original Movie called *The Price of a Broken Heart*. The story, inspired by actual events, was about a marriage shattered by infidelity and a wife who refused to play the victim. I love fact-based movies, especially ones that involve landmark legal battles.

Nearing the end of the movie, I realized that I had not spoken with Matt all day. I made myself a cup of hot tea with lemon in it for my sore throat and hit speed dial on my phone.

The call went to voice mail, and I left him a cute little message. "Hi, honey, it's raining here. Weezer and I are watching, what else, a chic flick. Actually, this movie is based on a true story about a businessman who cheats on his wife, and the wife sues the mistress for *Alienation of Affection.* I guess you could say that this is an educational weekend for me. So, if some young flight attendant ever decides to set her sights on you, she had better look out because the mistress was ordered to pay the ex-wife a huge civil settlement, and I will be just as ruthless. Bye"

I chuckled and hung up. "Matt will get a kick out of that," I told Weezer, while snuggling up with him under the chenille throw.

CHAPTER 19

With the sun shining in my eyes and a cat walking on my stomach, I realized that I had fallen asleep on the sofa, and that is where I had remained throughout the night.

"Yes, I will feed you right now," I told Weezer, as I sat up and stretched. Glancing at the time on my phone, I saw that it was eight o'clock. Once on my feet, I was pleasantly surprised to discover that the sore throat and fever had subsided. I felt like a new person.

"Wow, I slept fifteen hours," I said to the cat. "Obviously that's what I needed."

After feeding Weezer, I listened to the two messages that had been left on my phone since Friday evening. The first call was from IRS Supervisor Rick Moore reminding me that the second polygraph was set for Monday morning. The next message was from Paige, who was talking about getting together with Julie on Saturday afternoon. Strangely, there were no calls from Matt. It was either too late or too early for him to call between flights.

I leisurely enjoyed my Saturday morning cup of coffee while reviewing more bank records for Julie's case. At nine o'clock, I returned Paige's call. "I fell asleep early last night and slept straight through til this morning."

"I just wanted to see if you wanted to meet me and Julie at Chili's around one o'clock?"

"I would love to. See you then." I wandered into the bedroom and rummaged around in the nightstand drawer looking for the television remote control. I turned on the *Today Show* and was about to close the drawer when I saw the one hundred and sixty-seven dollar cell phone bill that I had asked Matt about.

I knew it was a billing error. But what got added that

caused such an increase in charges from one month to the next? I decided to compare the old statements to the current one.

I dumped a box containing personal bills and receipts onto the bed and began sorting through them. In the stack of paper, I found old AT&T statements for our home phone, but only one of Matt's detailed cell phone statements from six months earlier. Not unusual. Matt was not a stickler for keeping receipts. So, like a good investigator, I went in search of answers.

Dialing the number on the bill, I questioned the representative about the billing error.

"There was no error or adjustment that I can see," the representative said. "It looks like a portion of the bill, sixty-seven dollars, was paid by check, and one hundred dollars was remitted in cash at our Wiles Road location." The representative paused. "Mrs. Weber, I do not see your name listed on the account. Your husband's name is the only one I have on file, so I am afraid that I cannot provide you with any more information."

Confused, I hung up the phone and looked in our checkbook. Sure enough, there it was, a check issued to the phone company for the smaller amount. Then, looking online at our bank account, I found a one hundred dollar ATM withdrawal the very same day. I felt sick to my stomach. Matt had lied. He had some long and rather expensive conversations with someone that he didn't want me to know about.

At lunch, I told Paige and Julie that Matt had lied about the phone bill. I wanted advice. Paige and Julie were both divorced.

With a mixed drink in hand, Paige got straight to the point. "If you questioned Matt about seeing someone and offered him a chance to come clean, why wouldn't he take it? Unless nothing is going on."

Julie laughed. "Haven't you heard the saying he wants

to have his cake and eat it too? I'm no expert, but I don't think most men are going to admit to cheating unless they are caught in the act with pictures, a video, or documentary evidence."

Paige retorted, "Or maybe he didn't want Jennifer to bitch at him about running up such a huge phone bill, so he lied and said it was an error. I just can't see Matt cheating. He seems so happy."

"Maybe he's so happy because he has Jenn and some stranger on the side," Julie replied.

My phone rang. Looking at the caller id, I said, "It's him."

I answered the call, and in a tone dripping with honey, said, "Hi, babe. Are you still getting home around six o'clock?"

"I doubt it," Matt replied. "We've been hitting bad weather and experiencing flight delays, but I'll call when I get to Atlanta and know more."

"Be safe," I said, "and keep me posted."

Not a unusual occurrence in the airline industry, but once again, I had a sinking feeling that something was not right.

"Flight delays?" Paige asked as she picked at her salad.

I nodded and helped myself to some of the appetizers that had arrived at the table.

Julie speared a chicken tender and an egg roll. "Paige and I are thinking about taking in a movie tonight. If Matt doesn't get back until late, do you want to join us?"

"Maybe," I said, trying to shake the uneasy feeling I had.

After we had finished lunch, Paige suggested a little shopping at the nearby mall. Three hours later, and still not knowing if Matt was going to make it home on time or not, I had convinced the two women to come over to my house until I heard back from him.

At my house, Paige went straight into the office. "I'm going to get on your computer to see what movies are playing nearby."

"Find a comedy," Julie said as she walked past the office toward the kitchen. "I want to see something funny. I think all three of us need a good laugh tonight, and I need a drink of water. Those egg rolls were really salty."

I dropped my purse on the kitchen counter, and my cell phone rang. Listening to Matt, who was on the other end of the phone, I held a glass under the spigot and handed it to Julie.

Ending the call, I sadly looked at Julie. "Matt explained that the weather has not cooperated and he will most likely miss his flight from Atlanta to Ft. Lauderdale tonight."

The butterflies were back, fluttering all around in my stomach.

Coming to Matt's defense, Julie said, "You know, it's not his fault."

I nodded in agreement. "I know, but something is not right. I just have a feeling about this. You know with the phone bill and all."

Paige walked in and grabbed a bottle of water from the refrigerator. "What's not right?"

Julie shook her head in disbelief and snickered. "It's not right that I'm drinking warm tap water when Jenn has cold bottled water in her refrigerator."

Seeing how upset I was, Julie provided Paige with more information. "Jenn thinks Matt is not coming home tonight so he can be with some other woman."

Paige looked confused. "How do you equate weather delays with cheating?"

I took an airline schedule from the kitchen drawer. "There have been too many things that don't add up." I looked over the schedule. "This shows the La Guardia flight departing at 7:05 p.m. and arriving in Atlanta at 9:00 p.m. I'm going to call the airline at 9:15 to see if the La Guardia flight arrived on time in Atlanta. If Matt tells me that he got to Atlanta late and missed his flight to Ft. Lauderdale then I'll know he's lying and either staying in Atlanta to be with someone there or he is spending the night with her here in Ft. Lauderdale."

Concerned, Julie asked, "You think he's lying to you about flying in here tonight?"

"Yes," I replied. "And if he does lie to me about being on that flight, I want to be at the airport to see who he's with or where he's going."

"That's crazy." Julie looked over at Paige for support.

Paige remained calm. "Okay, let's say he is doing what you suspect. Why would you want to see that?"

My emotional dam burst and the reality of that question caused tears to roll down my face. "Because with everything else that's going on, I can't believe this, too, is happening. But I will believe it if I see it. I thought he loved me, but I don't know anything anymore."

Julie tried to comfort me, but I shrugged off her hug. "I know he's seeing someone. I feel it. And my gut says he's doing it tonight. He has an excuse for everything. But there is no excuse for him being in Ft. Lauderdale after he tells me he's not coming home."

The two women decided to stay with me until they could figure out what was going on. Julie and Paige watched television while I watched the clock.

Just after nine o'clock, I called the airline. "Has fight number 951, scheduled to depart La Guardia airport around seven o'clock, arrived in Atlanta?"

Paige and Julie glared at me, waiting for the answer.

I hung up the phone. "It landed in Atlanta at 9:08 p.m.," I said despondently. "If he says he missed the ten o'clock flight from Atlanta to Ft. Lauderdale, I want to be at the airport to see if he lied so he could spend the night with someone in Atlanta or if he is seeing someone here in

Florida."

Julie sat up in the loveseat. "Jenn, we don't even know that he's coming into Ft. Lauderdale tonight. Isn't it possible that he landed at one end of the airport and the Ft. Lauderdale flight was clear down at the other end of the terminal, and even if he ran all the way, he wouldn't make the flight?"

"I know it's a long shot," I said. "But his flight from New York landed minutes ago. It would not take him forty-five minutes to make it from one end of the concourse to the other. He lied to spend the night with this person in Atlanta or here. It's one or the other, Julie."

Skeptical, Julie said, "What if he landed, but his gate was not available? That happened to me. They left us sitting out there on the tarmac for quite a while. I almost missed my connecting flight."

Paige, once again, put the whole thing into perspective. "Okay, let's take this one step at a time and see what he has to say when he calls."

Just before ten o'clock, the phone rang. I answered, hoping and praying that I was wrong. "Hi, honey. Please tell me you're coming home tonight."

"No, I'm sorry," Matt replied. "They already pulled away from the gate and there are no other flights out of here tonight."

A tear rolled down my cheek. Paige looked over at Julie. The realization that Matt would prefer to spend the night with another woman rather than coming home to me cut me to the core.

"It's late and we couldn't have done anything tonight," he explained. "I'll sleep here on a couch in the crew room so I can hop on the 6 a.m. flight tomorrow and be home before you even wake up. Listen, I'm just about to jump on the tram to get some food in terminal B and I might lose you. So, I'll just see you in the morning."

I hung up the phone, reeling from the shock, and called the airline again. "Could you tell me what time flight

231 is scheduled to depart Atlanta and arrive in Ft. Lauderdale tonight? And if my friend misses that flight, when is the next flight from Atlanta to Ft. Lauderdale?"

I hung up the phone. "He's on that flight," I announced to the women. "He wanted to get off the phone with me because the Ft. Lauderdale flight was boarding. He also told me that he would catch the 6:00 a.m. flight to Ft. Lauderdale tomorrow morning. But the representative said the next flight to Ft. Lauderdale departs from Atlanta at 8:25 a.m. tomorrow."

Julie looked at the airline schedule on the counter. "I wonder why he thought there was a 6 a.m. flight?"

"Maybe that is the weekday schedule," Paige said. "He probably didn't know that it was different on weekends."

Julie shook her head in disbelief. "Stupid man. Stupid, stupid man."

"He's on tonight's flight," I said. "His plan is to get up from someone's bed at six tomorrow morning and drive home. I want to know whose bed he will be leaving."

Not sure what to do, Paige said, "Okay, if we agree to go to the airport, tell us what you have in mind if we see him."

"Nothing," I replied, glancing back and forth between Paige's grim expression and Julie's cynical glare. "I swear I'm not going to do anything. I've had a bad feeling about so many things lately. I just need to know the truth."

"We're not going to confront them, right?" Paige said rather sternly.

With tears flowing, I nodded. "I promise. I just need to know what's going on."

CHAPTER 20

Outside the Ft. Lauderdale airport terminal, I sat silently in the passenger seat of Paige's car, glancing at my watch every two minutes, waiting for the Atlanta flight to land. I prayed my instincts were wrong.

Julie waited in her vehicle outside of the employee parking lot where she had located Matt's car. On the push-to-talk or walkie-talkie feature of her Nextel cell phone, Julie reached out to Paige. "A plane flew over my location. We should know something soon enough."

Paige replied. "We'll keep you advised."

"I hope I'm wrong," I whispered.

"Me too," Paige said. "And when you are wrong, you will owe Julie and me a really expensive dinner. I'm thinking Fleming's Steakhouse."

I saw movement inside the terminal. My heart rate accelerated.

Paige raised the binoculars to her eyes. "So, the majority of the passengers will take the escalator down one level to baggage claim, but Matt will stay on this level, right?" She paused. "Wait, I see a guy. No, that's not Matt."

I relaxed my tense body. It felt good to think I was wrong about the situation.

"How about now? Is that Matt?"

"I can't tell." My heart was almost pounding out of my chest.

Paige handed me the binoculars and pushed the button on her phone to talk to Julie. "Hey, we may have spotted him. Stand by."

The man looked like Matt from a distance, but I wasn't sure it was him. Adjusting the binoculars, I squeezed my eyes shut numerous times and watched him light a cigarette. Icy fingers closed around my heart and squeezed. "That can't be," I mumbled in disbelief.

Paige grabbed the binoculars away from me and pinged Julie on the Nextel. "Well, she was right. He's here." Handing the binoculars back to me, Paige put Julie on speaker phone.

"What is he doing?" Julie asked.

"Smoking a cigarette and it appears that he's waiting for the employee bus," Paige replied.

A dense fog fell over my life. In shock, I mumbled, "I don't know this guy at all."

Julie replied. "What did she say? Is Jenn alright?"

Paige looked over at me. "I'll have to get back to you on that one."

Julie chuckled. "I didn't know he smoked."

"From her reaction, neither did Jennifer," Paige replied, still looking through the binoculars. "Okay, it looks like he's calling someone on his cell phone."

I felt energized again. "Let it be me."

With her free hand, Paige reached into her purse and handed me a tiny, unopened bottle of liquor. Without hesitation and without looking to see what it was, I chugged it. Then I pulled my phone from my pocket and willed it to ring. *Matt wasn't cheating on me. He somehow got a last minute flight home and was calling me to explain the situation.*

Paige spotted lights in her rearview mirror. "Okay Julie, the employee bus is coming up behind us, so we should be at your location within minutes."

"You know where to find me," Julie pleasantly replied.

We watched Matt hop on the bus. Paige passed her phone to me as we pulled away from the terminal. "I thought that drink might come in handy. I have more where that came from."

My cell phone remained silent in my shaking hand.

"No, I'll wait." Still hopeful that Matt would call me. I made sure I had a signal and checked my ring volume.

Paige followed the bus to the employee parking lot, and said to Julie, "I'll cover the exit on the west side of the lot, just in case it's open."

"You have an eyeball on his car?" I asked Julie.

Perturbed, Julie replied, "His car has not been out of my sight for a second, Jenn."

Paige positioned her vehicle at the opposite end of the road from where Julie was parked and in a location where we could not see Matt's vehicle.

Anxious to know what was happening, I said to Julie, "He should have reached his car by now. Are you watching the right car?"

Frustrated, Julie replied, "Jenn, they're all just now getting to their cars. Give it a minute. Okay, I see him. He's here. He should be pulling out momentarily. It looks like all the cars are exiting the east end of the lot. So, the exit down by you must be closed."

Minutes passed. I bit my lower lip, dry and cracked. *Maybe he decided it was too late to call me and hung up before the first ring. He could be home in twenty minutes.*

"It looks like he's just sitting there," Julie reported. "Maybe he's having second thoughts."

I inhaled deeply and prayed that Matt did change his mind about whatever this was and that he would drive home. Again, I glared at my phone. *Ring.*

Finally Julie said, "I'm going to see if I can get a better view."

The next thing Paige and I heard was Julie laughing. "You're going to love this. He's got a flat tire."

Paige and I burst into laughter. It was the first time in days that I had a good laugh.

"Talk about poetic justice," Julie shouted.

"Now what is he doing?" I impatiently asked.

Still laughing, Julie said, "It looks like he's changing

the tire. In record time, I might add." She paused. "Okay, I see taillights. Here we go."

My pulse raced. I desperately wanted another bottle of liquid courage, but I restrained myself.

Matt's car darted from the employee lot and turned east. Julie had the eyeball and followed about four car lengths behind. Paige tried to catch up, but Julie and Matt were moving so fast it was going to take time.

Still on speaker, Julie called out the next turn. "We're making a right on Airport Drive."

At least a half-mile ahead of Paige, Julie shouted in the phone, "He's driving like a bat out of hell. Does he always drive this fast?"

Paige gunned the gas in an attempt to catch Julie.

"Matt turned east on Hollywood Boulevard," Julie reported. "I clocked him at sixty miles per hour in a forty mile per hour speed zone."

A sob escaped my lips. That wasn't the direction of our home.

Frantically calling out the next turn, Julie said, "Now we're making a left on U.S. One and, if it is at all possible, he's going even faster."

Paige sped up. "I'm right behind you." No sooner had she said that than Julie called out another change in direction.

"We're turning right down some side street. I didn't catch the name of the street. Did you see my brake lights where I turned?"

I pointed ahead. "Next right."

Paige whipped onto the street, almost rear-ending Julie's stopped vehicle in the center of the deserted road.

Still on speaker, Julie said, "I don't know where he went. I made the right, and he was gone."

Paige looked around the residential neighborhood. "Maybe he pulled into one of these driveways." She backed her car up. Both she and I looked down each driveway, while Julie drove up to the intersecting street and turned left. "I'm sorry Jenn, but we lost him."

"He went to Embassy Suites on 17th Street Causeway," I said. "Matt once told me that's where the airline crews stay."

"On my way," Julie replied.

As Paige pulled into the hotel parking lot, Julie came back on speakerphone. "You were right again. He parked in the rear and ran in through a back door."

"A few months ago Joel thought he saw Matt at the Crab Shack across the street from here," I said. "Matt denied it. I now know Joel wasn't mistaken."

Paige parked in a space next to Julie's car and opened the car windows. "How fast were you going?" Paige asked.

Julie laughed. "I hit sixty-five a few times on some residential streets. Thank God no police were around. We'd have a lot of explaining to do."

The three of us sat for a long minute until Julie broke the silence. "Now what?"

I shrugged my shoulders. "Now nothing. He's going to tell me he was in Atlanta, when I know that he is screwing some flight attendant here."

Julie rubbed her temple. "Jenn, I'm really sorry."

I shook my head, thinking about how stupidly trusting I was of Matt. "Remember that grocery store parking lot sex dream I told you two about? My subconscious must have picked up on something back then."

"I remember how mad you said he got," Julie replied. "Probably because he thought you were on to him. I think you should tell him about another dream where instead of being stranded at the airport he's having sex in a hotel."

Paige rolled her eyes. "I think we should get out of here." She exited the parking lot and handed me another bottle of liquor, which I again chugged.

CHAPTER 21

I wandered into my house and looked around. It didn't seem like a place where I had lived the last three years. Everything was different. Nothing would ever be the same.
Paige was my shadow. "I'm sorry I didn't believe you."

In a daze, I walked into the office and sank into the chair at my desk. With a whole array of thoughts tugging at my every emotion, I leaned back and closed my eyes.

Paige flopped onto the sofa behind me. "Those hang-up calls from a blocked number. Could it have been this woman that Matt's with?"

I swiveled around to face her. "Maybe. I don't know," I said, with tears streaming down my face. "That would mean that Matt had let me live in fear over the last two months, believing a drug kingpin was threatening my life. That would make him a coward and a monster." I wiped my face with the back of my hand and dug into a pile of papers on the desk. I found the Verizon phone bill and punched a number into my phone.

Exhausted, Paige moaned, "What are you doing?"

I covered the mouthpiece of the phone. "I'm going to see if I can get some information about who he's with at the hotel."

Paige put her arms over her eyes. "It's after midnight. Don't you get enough of this shit at work?"

I ignored her and asked the Verizon representative some questions about the bill.

"The numbers being called are outside of your calling area," the man explained. "That's why it's more expensive. It also looks like we could cut your bill in half if we signed you up for unlimited texting."

"Texting?" I mumbled. I felt the slow, radiating throb of dread as I jotted down the numbers that the representative said were causing the problems. I thanked the man and hung up.

Barely awake, Paige heard tapping on the computer keyboard. "Now what are you doing?"

"Searching the Internet for the phone numbers the representative provided." A minute later, I handed Paige a printout with the results. "I need you to call one of these numbers for me."

She rubbed her eyes and looked at the number I had circled on the paper. "You think this is her? And more importantly, are you sure you want to do this?"

Staring at the floor, I nodded.

Paige made the call. Through weary apologetic eyes, she looked over at me. After a minute, she hung up. "I got a voice mail for a woman named Liv."

"Olivia Ogden," I said weakly. "That's the name that came up when I ran the Florida tags on that car the real estate agent saw in the driveway of our Atlanta house."

Paige arched a brow. "I guess that's good news. It means that it wasn't Londono's people up there casing your property. It was this Olivia woman looking for Matt." Paige sat up. "When something is not right in our lives, we know it, and you knew. You just thought it was Londono, not this."

"I don't know why she has a vehicle with a Florida license plate, but I can tell you that Matt's phone bill has been high because he's been calling her residence in Atlanta and texting her cell phone, also an Atlanta number."

Paige stood up and stretched. "And, you think that's who he's with at the hotel?"

"Most likely, unless he's cheating on her as well."

"Now that we know he's cheating and with whom, do you want to stay here and confront him in the morning or do you want to come home with me and get your thoughts together?"

Tired and wanting to think, I packed an overnight bag of clothes, jumped in my car, and followed Paige to her house.

Because Matt was preoccupied with his girlfriend, I knew he would not answer his phone. I left him a message telling him that I had to drive up to Orlando early in the morning to follow a lead on a case, and that I wouldn't be home for a few days.

Hurt and angry, hearing Matt's voice mail message, I wanted to scream into the phone. I hate you! How could you do this? My thoughts then turned to revenge. After all the anguish Matt had put me through, he and his girlfriend deserved a taste of their own medicine. My first thought involved a report of a kidnapping and a SWAT team storming the hotel room. *No, too much work. That would require the purchase of a burner phone in the middle of the night.*

***

The alarm clock buzzed, awakening me from a horrible nightmare. I shot straight up out of bed, gasping, as if I had been resuscitated back to life after being pulled from a dark body of frigid water. Looking around the unfamiliar room, the painful events from the prior evening flooded back.

Paige tapped on the bedroom door. "I'm so sorry about the alarm clock."

Feeling mentally numb, my voice cracked. "It's amazing how your whole world can change so quickly. The contrast between my life before last night and now is so stark that it seems like an entirely different existence."

Paige offered a sympathetic smile. "I understand. Take your time getting up. There are fresh towels in the guest bathroom, and I'll make us some coffee. Come down when you feel like it."

I saw no point in staying in bed torturing myself with thoughts about Matt and the other woman waking up together and having morning sex. *Maybe a shower will help.* It didn't. Just the opposite, the shower stall served more as a sanctuary where all of my heartbreak, fears, and anger came gushing out like the forceful jets of water beating against my bare skin. The wet spray pounding against the glass shower door and the wall tiles barely masked the uncontrollable sobbing sounds coming from within.

I took my time drying my hair and getting dressed. *It's not like I can go home. I certainly don't want to risk running into Matt after telling him I went to Orlando.*

Downstairs, coffee and a full breakfast were sitting on the kitchen counter. "Did you get some sleep?" Paige asked.

I gazed around her kitchen as if it were my first time seeing it. The trendy apple red blender, tucked neatly into a corner of the counter, evoked memories of happier times and all the margarita parties Paige had hosted. *How Matt loved those parties.*

I poured myself a cup of coffee. "Not much, maybe a few hours."

Paige pushed a bottle of pills across the counter. "They're sleeping pills. If you think you need them, start out with half of one tonight and see how that works. But, no alcohol."

Paige knew firsthand how painful and unsettling marital problems could be. Although her ex-husband didn't cheat on her, he did put her through hell over custody disputes.

Slumped in a chair, I sipped my coffee and checked my messages. I was surprised to have one from Matt so early in the morning. He apologized for not getting home the previous night and said he hoped that he would see me before his next trip on Tuesday.

"You should have just busted him at the hotel, rather than putting up with this bullshit," Paige commented, turning to the community section of the newspaper.

I fantasized about how amusing it would have been to

pretend that I was room service, only to squirt Matt and his whore in the face with pepper spray. I chuckled as I searched through the telephone book on the counter.

Paige put down the paper and watched me out of curiosity.

I found what I was looking for, punched a number into the phone, and said to the person on the other end of the line, "Good morning, could you please connect me to a room registered to Olivia Ogden?"

Paige's eyes widened like saucers. She stared at me in utter disbelief.

"Oh shoot," I coyly replied. "She has something of mine. Maybe I can catch her at the airport. Do you know what time she checked out?"

I ended the call and raised my eyebrows at Paige.

"Let me guess, she checked out just before six this morning."

"Yep. If they would have connected me to her room, I would have hung up. I just wanted to see if that was the woman he was with last night."

"You think he's seeing multiple women?" Paige asked inquisitively.

"I don't know. Hell, I'm just the clueless wife who, until yesterday, thought I was his one and only. Now, I'm playing catch-up."

"Well, now we know how he came up with that six in the morning flight time. It was her flight that was leaving so early."

"The idiot didn't do his research," I replied. "If he had, he would have discovered that there were no flights from Atlanta to Ft. Lauderdale at that hour."

"He didn't expect you to check up on him," Paige said as she handed me a business card. "This attorney represented me in my divorce. I think you should call him. He's very good."

Hearing the word divorce, the butterflies returned to

my stomach. I didn't know if I was going to cry, throw up, or both.

Paige rubbed my arm. "I hate seeing you like this. What pisses me off most is that Matt saw how worried you were about the phone calls, yet he said nothing and did nothing to make it stop. Hell, even the cigarettes were Matt's, and rather than own up to having a bad habit, he let you think that a person was watching the house, and worse, stalking you. So, my question to you is this. Are you going to be able to forgive him for doing those things?"

What Paige said made a lot of sense. I needed to think long and hard about how I felt about what Matt had done, and what my next move would be. *Can I ever trust him again?* I wondered. *Do I want to try to work this out through marriage counseling or just initiate legal proceedings?*

I thought about how humiliated I was going to be telling friends and co-workers who had been worried about my safety, that what was happening appeared to have been a hoax perpetrated by my cowardly cheating husband and his insecure slutty girlfriend.

Late in the morning, Julie called to see how I was doing. Paige provided an update. "Jennifer found the girlfriend's name, address, and phone number sometime after midnight. Then this morning she contacted Embassy Suites and discovered that it was the girlfriend's flight leaving Ft. Lauderdale at six. All in all, I would say it has been a very productive morning. As for this afternoon or evening, I have no idea what tricks she has up her sleeve."

Rarely moving from the large comfy living room chair I had curled into, I spent the remainder of Sunday reflecting on the lies my husband had told me. "An affair was something that we could have possibly survived," I told Paige, who settled into the sofa opposite me, "but he allowed it to take on a life of its own. Then there was his total lack of respect for me and our relationship. Matt and his girlfriend must have laughed over the whole thing. It was no wonder

Matt got angry and defensive when I wanted to trace our incoming calls."

"He probably shit himself," Paige said. "But he deserved it for not ending the affair or even putting it on hold while we were dealing with what we thought was a potentially dangerous situation. I'm thinking about talking to Mullaney about bringing criminal charges against Matt for impeding a federal investigation."

I nodded in agreement and pulled up my contact list on my cell phone.

Paige watched. "Please tell me you're not calling Matt."

I looked at her incredulously. "I'm calling our Atlanta realtor, who I've become friends with." After I heard the beep, I said, "Robin, this is Jennifer Weber. I discovered that Matt is seeing a woman with an Atlanta phone number and Florida tags on her car. Can you line up a locksmith so I can throw a monkey wrench into Matt's love life at our new home?"

I hung up, feeling swallowed up by a dull numbness. "What really hurts is that Matt didn't care that the calls, and everything he and his girlfriend did, upset me. How can I ever forgive a man who cared more about the sex he was getting from some cheap whore than the pain he was causing his wife and partner of seven years?"

"Sounds like you have answered your own question," Paige replied.

CHAPTER 22

At nine o'clock, I found AUSA Robert Mullaney pacing in the hall outside a room at FBI headquarters where my polygraph exam was to be administered.

Hearing my approach, he scornfully glanced at me before refocusing on the examiner, who was setting up his equipment behind the thick, insulated soundproof window. "I gave the examiner my list of questions. If even one of them comes back inconclusive, I will have your badge."

As Mullaney walked away, I called after him, "Thanks for the vote of confidence." I then tapped on the door to advise the examiner that I had arrived.

The polygraph examiner had me take a seat in the one empty chair in the small room, and face a blank white wall. While placing various measuring devices around my midsection, arms, and fingers to record changes in my blood pressure, respiration, and skin conductivity, the man explained the importance of answering truthfully.

The examiner then took a seat behind me at the desk where the small machine had been positioned. He began with the pre-test interview questions to gain preliminary information. "Is your name Jennifer?" he asked. "Do you reside in Florida?"

Next, a "stim test" was conducted, and I was told to answer untruthfully so the tester could measure my response to a lie. "Do you have black hair?" he asked in a monotone voice.

"Yes," I responded. "Am I wearing a red shirt?" he asked, again in the same unvaried tone.

"Yes," I replied, knowing his shirt was blue.

After a series of questions like those, the examiner advised me that the actual test was going to begin.

Some of the questions asked were irrelevant, others were diagnostic questions, and most were the important questions that the AUSA was interested in having answered.

For nearly an hour, I could feel Mullaney staring at the back of my head while the examiner alternated between the different types of questions. When the exam was over, the straight-faced, pear-shaped examiner said, "AUSA Mullaney asked me to text him, and only him, the results. So, you are free to go."

After turning in my visitor's badge to the receptionist in the main lobby of the building, I called IRS Supervisor Moore to advise him that I had taken the test, and that the examiner had refused to share the results with anyone but Mullaney.

"Alright, get your ass back here," Moore said. "I'll give it an hour and call Mullaney to see if we need to arrest you or put you back to work."

I liked Moore's undaunted attitude in such a serious situation. *Mullaney is too tightly wound*, I thought as I drove to the IRS office. *He probably beats up old ladies in his spare time, just so he can bring his "A" game to the office.*

Arriving at my office, I wanted to focus on something other than the polygraph results, so I began flipping through the bank records that had just arrived. Londono's trial was almost finished, but what could it hurt to do a little snooping regarding Rosa's mother. After all, wasn't it my comments about her that upset Rosa so much she wanted to have me killed.

My heart skipped a beat as soon as I saw the opening deposit ticket and supporting document showing a transfer from a Bahamian bank. The account had been opened three years earlier with a thirty thousand dollar deposit, which coincided with the time frame when Rosa and Londono became an item. Knowing Rosa's financial situation as I did, I suspected that the money came from Londono. Rummaging through files, I found a copy of an interview that agents conducted early on with Rosa's mother. The mother stated that she was entirely dependent on and supported by Rosa. So where did these funds come from, and why didn't the mother mention this account or deposit if it was legitimately hers?

I was on to something, and so far, all my instincts about people had been correct. The most significant clue connecting the account to Londono was that Rosa's mother closed the account days after Rosa's death, and rather than just transferring the funds to another account, she took the remaining twenty-one thousand dollars out in cash.

An hour later, I was called into IRS Supervisor Rick Moore's office. AUSA Mullaney was already there, an ominous sign. Mullaney was probably present so he could deliver the bad news, videotape my termination, and leak it to the media. I walked into the office, determined not to succumb to any more mental abuse from another man.

"Before either of you say anything, I have something I want to tell you." I briefed them on my recent discovery about Matt and hoped that they would have mercy on me and fire me without too many theatrics.

To my surprise, Mullaney was sympathetic to my plight and after hearing my story, provided me with good news. "You passed the polygraph and all the financial information you provided checked out. So, there will be no criminal charges, but because of Londono's allegations about the drugs which his attorney brought up, we still can't have you or Steve participating in the trial."

"Fine with me. The less I see Londono, the better I will feel."

"Are we sure that the calls you and your husband received had nothing to do with Londono?" Moore asked me.

"Not a clue," I replied.

"No, we're not," Mullaney said. "The DEA agent pulled phone records that indicated that some of the earlier calls were placed from locations in Miami." Mullaney paused. "I hate to sound insensitive, but hopefully Matt was seeing someone who resided in Miami, and the calls were personal and had nothing to do with Londono. Also, we have no way of knowing if Londono was behind the attempted break in at your house."

Moore shrugged. "Okay, well, I guess that means you still need to keep your guard up. If convicted on the charges, Londono may want revenge even though his attorney has been advised that you and Steve are no longer on the case."

Mullaney turned to me and added, "With us nearing the end of the trial you should have no more trouble, but if you do, let me know immediately."

What it came down to was the threat that Londono posed was unresolved. But, looking at my watch, it was time to resolve my other problem.

I jumped in my car and drove down to Hollywood for my meeting with Paige's divorce attorney. With a storm of confusion and heart ache brewing inside me, I turned on the radio as a distraction. What did I hear? Cher. "*Do you believe in life after love? I can feel something inside me say I really don't think you're strong enough.*" Familiar with the song, I sadly sang along, "*What am I supposed to do, sit around and wait for you? Well, I can't do that, and there's no turning back.*" My throat tightened, and the tears started to flow as I sang, "*I need time... to move on. I need a love... to feel strong. I've had time to think it through, and... maybe I'm too good for you.*"

Through the tears, I slapped at the buttons on the dash and silenced the radio. I felt emptiness inside and thought about my mother. With all I was going through, I had a new found appreciation for her strength and intelligence. I only wish she was alive for me to tell her that. She was a woman who had dreams of a happily ever after marriage. Unfortunately, her dreams were crushed by heartache not once, but three times.

At age twenty, Mary, my mother, married a wonderful man and had my two half brothers. When the boys were ages three and five, their father died of cancer. In order to pay the rent on their apartment, and keep food on the table, my mother got two jobs. She was a secretary by day, and a cocktail waitress at night.

She told me about the months after her first husband's death, how in the throes of grief, she was faced with the reality that she was broke due to a staggering amount of debt owed to the doctors and hospital. She once said she would not have made it through those years if it hadn't of been for her two sisters who helped care for the boys while they were young.

Twenty years later, my mother met my father and found love once again. I was told that Claude was a wonderful, loving husband and father. I was a surprise to the couple. At age thirty-nine, Mary didn't think she could get pregnant, but she did. Old home movies show two people in love and enjoying life with their new baby girl.

But all that ended three years later when Claude died of a heart attack. "I felt as though I'd been punched in the stomach," she told me. She was financially better off than she had been when her first husband died. This time she owned the house we lived in, and it was nearly paid off. However, once again, she was a single woman raising a baby. My half brothers were in their twenties and away in the armed forces.

Because she wasn't flush with money, my mother would have to get a job and seek daycare for me. "I couldn't go through it all over again," she explained to me when I was seventeen.

Mary wed my stepfather, Paul, within a year of my father's death, not for love, but for security. Paul had a good job with Goodyear, a nice house, and liked children. He was nice to me, but not so nice to my mother. Their relationship started off warm and hospitable. "I thought I would learn to love him," she said. Unfortunately, as the years passed, the marriage, based on convenience, turned to discontent and eventually to hostility and bitterness on both their parts. Paul and Mary divorced. Paul was financially well off, but somehow Mary got nothing in the settlement. "I was depressed and just didn't have the energy to fight for assets," my mother said.

I pulled myself together upon arriving at the attorney's office. I wiped the black streaks of mascara from my face before introducing myself to the man and providing him with the documents he had requested.

"The Atlanta house was purchased with money from my mother," I explained. "It was in my name and Matt's, but after a heated argument a few months back, Matt Quit Claimed the property over to me."

The attorney looked over the document and smiled. "It's good for you that he did that."

I reflected back on that day. Matt had dropped me off at an Atlanta mall to shop for home furnishings. He hated shopping and said he had some paperwork to catch up on at the airport. Two hours later, I called him a message asking him to pick me up. My calls went unanswered. He returned my call and picked me up four hours later, claiming that he left his cell phone in his car at the employee lot and figured that I would need at least four hours to get everything done. I should have known it was another woman. Where were my instincts and investigative skills then?

"What about the Florida house?" the attorney asked, bringing me back to the present.

I stared out the window. "Same thing. Matt said he didn't care about assets."

The attorney chuckled. "I guess we'll soon see if he still feels that way. How soon can you have him in here?"

"Maybe Monday. He's returning from a trip on Saturday, so we should be able to meet with you that next weekday morning."

"I can see how difficult this is for you," the attorney said. "If you prefer, I can meet with Matt alone. You are in no way required to attend this meeting. I will review the Divorce

Agreement with him, and if we run into any snags, I will call you. If not, once it is signed by him, it will become a binding contract that I will file with the court."

I nodded and got up from the chair. "That would be nice. Once I tell him that I know about the infidelity, I have no desire to ever see him again."

"Understood," the attorney said. "I'm also concerned about your well being. Do you have a friend or family you can stay with until this is over?"

"I have friends. Good friends who are helping me get through this."

After the meeting, I no longer felt like the victim of a hit-and-run accident. Sure, I was hurt, and I wasn't my cheerful, confident self. But I was finally nearing the end of the charade. Matt would be home in a few days, I would confront him, and my marriage would be over.

CHAPTER 23

Paige's dining room was used as a makeshift office where I spent most of Tuesday analyzing bank records, preparing spreadsheets, and trying to keep my mind off Matt.

Steve and I were not involved in the trial, but we had not given up on finding more information that could add to what AUSA Mullaney already had.

A little before noon, Steve showed up with a lame story about dropping off paperwork for Paige. "These are the phone records from Londono's right-hand man's disposable phone. Mullaney wants her to go over these records tonight."

I cocked my head and shot Steve a suspicious look.

"Hey, what can I tell you? Paige wasn't at the office. So, I thought I would drop them off in person."

Judging by the serious look on his face, I suspected Paige had told him what had happened. "Who told you?" I asked.

"Am I that transparent?" He took a seat at the kitchen counter. "The only thing Paige told me was to be extra nice to you, and no pilot or flight attendant jokes. Mullaney is the one who gave me the details."

That's a shock, I thought. *Who says men don't gossip?*

"I'm trying to get my mind off it, but I can't concentrate," I admitted. "I look at a document and minutes later I have forgotten what I saw."

"How about a drive to the beach? Let's show pictures of Rosa and Londono to the concierge at some of the condominium complexes that agents have not hit. I know it's a long shot, but it'll get you out of the house and maybe we'll get lucky."

The remainder of the afternoon we drove along Ft. Lauderdale beach, talked about how men are pigs, and eliminated about six beachfront complexes from our list of potentials, before I received a late afternoon call from Laurel saying that Matt had left for his trip.

"Paige and some of my other friends are going to help me copy personal documents this evening, so can we call it an early day?" I asked Steve.

We drove in silence most of the way back to Paige's house, until Steve finally asked, "When are you going to tell Matt that you saw him?"

"As soon as I get my affairs in order," I replied. "No pun intended," I added as we pulled into her driveway.

My glum demeanor brightened on the short drive from Paige's home to my own. Not that I didn't appreciate Paige's generosity for allowing me to hide out in her lovely home, but I was anxious to sleep in my own bed again. *Matt will be gone for the next few days, and that's enough time for me to get my thoughts together regarding everything I want to tell him about how badly he hurt me.*

I pulled into my driveway, and my stomach clenched. Matt was standing in the front yard, blissfully pruning the palm trees. A smiled spread across his face. He walked over to the car and gave me a kiss.

I didn't have to act surprised at seeing him, because I was flabbergasted that he was still there. I put on my best pretend smile. "I thought you had a trip."

He took my overnight bag from the car, and cheerfully replied, "I did. However, my father decided to pay us a surprise visit. So, I changed my schedule to fly out tomorrow instead." He handed me the bag, and said, "I'm going to finish up out front here, and then I thought we could have my dad over for dinner, maybe throw something on the grill."

Still in a state of shock, all that came out of my mouth was, "Uh, I guess so."

Nervous, I staggered into the kitchen and heard a tapping sound. I looked down. Was it the heel of my foot on the wood floor? No, it was coming from the back of the house. It was Laurel, knocking at the patio door. I ran through the living room and slid the door open. "Did you see? He's still here."

Laurel was apologetic and wringing her hands. "I know. I feel awful. When I saw him drive off a few hours ago, I thought he was leaving for his trip. Then I heard something, and he was at the side of the house pruning."

I grabbed Laurel's hands to calm her. "It's alright. I screwed up too. His father made an impromptu visit to Florida, and I agreed to have him over for dinner tonight."

She pulled back. "What? Why did you agree to that?"

"He caught me off guard. I couldn't think fast enough to come up with a reason why we couldn't have him over."

Laurel shook her head. "How about saying I don't need to cook for your family any longer because I'm divorcing you?"

"I can't. I'm not ready. I want to have everything in place. I want to be prepared."

"I know," Laurel replied. "But how are you going to pull this off?"

"With lots of alcohol."

Laurel rubbed my arm. "You poor thing. Call me if you need anything. I'll call the other girls right now and tell them what's happening."

"It'll be alright," I said, wanting to believe my own words.

Laurel hugged me. "I know it will, but confront Matt soon. Acting like you don't know what he has done must be tearing you up inside."

It was.

A few hours later, Matt left the house and returned with his father and some nice looking steaks to throw on the grill. I was working on a salad when the two men walked in carrying wine and groceries. I had always liked Matt's father, Thomas, a heavy set man in his late sixties, retired from the securities industry, very intelligent and an excellent conversationalist.

"Hello Jennifer," Thomas said. "How is the U.S. government today?"

He loved chatting about politics and current events involving the government.

"In good shape," I replied.

The evening started out pleasantly enough, with Matt focusing most of his attention on his father, which I was thankful for. Periodically, Matt would pull me close and lovingly run his hand up and down my back. My instinct was to break his hand off at the wrist and shove it into his lying pie-hole. But instead, I played along with his romantic gestures, and then quickly scampered away, out of his reach. It was hard to do because there was a part of me that wanted to wrap my arms around him, to believe that he still loved me, in spite of what he had done.

I swallowed the last of my wine in one big gulp, wishing it were a magical elixir that would make me forget what I had discovered.

Minutes of small talk felt like hours, especially knowing that the entire evening was an act by both me and Matt. Wine made the situation bearable, except for when Matt would tell a story about sleeping at the airport or not being able to catch flights home.

Matt finally took the steaks out to the grill, and I remained in the kitchen, wondering how I was ever going to make it through the rest of the evening. *Maybe I should confront Matt in front of his father*, I thought. An inner response came back, *No, don't do that to Thomas. Just have another glass of wine.* With my stomach in knots, I finished my third glass of wine before dinner was even ready. I just wanted the night to end. I couldn't remember the last time I had eaten, but because I was so stressed out, I wasn't hungry.

When I saw Thomas setting the table, I retrieved the salad from the refrigerator and joined Matt and my soon to be ex-father-in-law on the patio.

"So, how's work going, Jennifer?" Thomas asked. He loved to hear about my job. "Anything you can share with us?"

In between bites, Matt said, "Tell him about the drug case that has been causing us so much grief."

Hearing the cool indifferent tone in Matt's voice made my blood boil. "A drug trafficker we arrested told the Colombian cartel that another agent and I stole their cocaine. If that wasn't stressful enough, we've also been receiving strange telephone calls, and there was an attempted break-in here at the house."

Thomas looked at Matt with great concern. Matt just rolled his eyes and stuck another piece of steak in his mouth.

"That's awful," Thomas said. "You could have been killed."

What I said next can only be blamed on the wine and the anger I felt toward Matt for all his cheating and lying. "Yes, but thankfully there has been a break in the case."

That piqued Matt's attention. "Really, what's that?"

Now, it was my turn to stick it to him. I could make up any story I wanted, and that is exactly what I did.

"The government's attorney subpoenaed Matt's and my phone records in order to charge the head of the organization with trying to intimidate or threaten a federal agent," I said, wondering if that was going to scare Matt into coming clean about the long conversations he had been having with his girlfriend. However, an admission was not all that I was after. I wanted Matt to feel the fear and the stress that I had experienced over the last few months.

The truth of the matter was that I was a woman scorned who wanted to watch her bastard husband squirm, so I added, "Even if the individual who had called us had used a disposable phone, we can trace the calls to the cell phone towers that were used and find the location of the person who made the call. On my way home today, I picked up the phone records from that trap and trace. We'll comb through them tomorrow and see what we find."

Enthralled by the conversation, Thomas asked, "Is a trap and trace a device to see who the criminals are calling? I thought things like that were all made up for the movies."

Hearing that news, Matt lost his appetite and pushed his plate aside. I was enjoying every minute of the charade. "In cases like this one, the government can obtain detailed phone records for incoming and outgoing calls."

Whether it was the alcohol or the knowledge that I now had the upper hand, I felt empowered and was thoroughly enjoying the tension and apprehension that was growing on Matt's face. "And because of everything that has been happening, the police are providing the government attorney with a video tape from the traffic camera at the intersection outside our development. That way we'll see what cars were in the area the night of the attempted break in."

Hearing that, Thomas became very concerned. "I had no idea all this was going on." He turned to his son. "Matt, why didn't you say something to your mother?"

Clearly unhinged, Matt excused himself from the table.

Mentally patting myself on the back, I knew that I had caused enough trouble for one night, so I changed the subject to Matt's grandmother. "Thomas, how is your mother?"

Thomas went with the flow. "She's as well as she can be at 90. As I was telling Matt, we're planning a party for her in March. Do you think the two of you can take time off work to visit?"

Matt returned to the table near the end of the conversation. Holding a bottle of wine, he seemed a little more composed and poured himself another drink.

I wanted to scream, "No, there are no more trips to California for us because your son is a skirt chasing cheating bastard." But, all that came out of my mouth was, "I would love to see Helen again, but I think Matt is going to have to take that trip without me."

Surprised and disappointed, Thomas looked at Matt, who ignored my comment. Sensing the tension between us, Tomas lit a cigarette, looked out at the lake, and said nothing more.

I stacked the dinner plates and strategically moved the ashtray closer to Matt. "Thomas, how long have you been a smoker?"

"All my life," he replied. "Forty or fifty years ago we did not know the negative effects cigarettes have on the body."

"I'm just surprised none of your children took up the habit," I commented.

"As am I," Thomas replied, proudly smiling at Matt.

Shit, I should have taken some pictures of Matt with a cigarette in his mouth. I could have sent them to the ex-in-laws after the divorce.

Matt hastily gathered the stack of plates and went inside. He picked up his cell phone and walked out of view.

Wanting to keep an eye on him, I gathered up a few serving bowls from the table. "I'll see if Matt wants some help inside."

Thomas, not wanting to get involved in the apparent marital drama, nodded and puffed away on his cigarette.

Inside, Matt was nowhere to be found. My best guess was that he was on the phone with his girlfriend, outside pacing on the front porch, and smoking a cigarette.

The thought that he was complaining to her about me was so unsettling that I ran into the bathroom and splashed cold water on the hot tears running down my face. It took a few minutes, but I finally pulled myself together.

Suddenly, Matt pounded on the door and growled, "I'm taking my dad home."

I quickly dried my face and raced out the front door to say goodbye to Thomas, but they were gone.

Back inside the house, I stared at the dirty plates and pans strewn across the kitchen counter. Outside, past the messy patio, the silver moonlight lit up the surface of the lake. I aimlessly wandered through my dimly lit house where decorative candles dripped hot wax onto the tops of the tables. I didn't care.

My head was pounding from the wine and the tension of the night. My body was shaking, inside and out. Matt had said that he would be back to clean up the mess, and that was exactly what I was going to let him do. It was high time he clean up his messes.

I went into the bathroom and took a valium. I needed to calm down if I wanted to have a meaningful conversation with Matt when he returned. Even if we didn't talk, I at least wanted to be composed. I turned off the bedroom light, laid down, and watched the candlelight shadows dance on the wall while listening for Matt's footsteps. *Should I confront him tonight or hold off until morning?* Soon, the cool softness of the bed swallowed me up.

CHAPTER 24

Hand in hand, Matt and I walked through a historic Norman castle in Wales. The view was of the Irish Sea. I felt the intense heat of the sun on my face and thought, this can't possibly be Wales. I turned to tell Matt that something was wrong, but choked on my words.

I climbed up through the layers of drug induced sleep and opened my eyes. Two feet from my face, flames shot up toward the ceiling. The lampshade was a raging inferno soaring up the bedroom wall. Struck with terror, I rolled away from the blaze toward Matt, attempting to wake him. I gasped for air and screamed out his name.

My eyes burned. I could barely see the other side of the bed through the thick smoke. I ran my hand across the comforter. Matt's side of the bed was empty, never slept in.

Horrified, I crawled away from the flames to the far end of the bed. My ears were ringing from a high-pitched screeching noise. *Water. I need to extinguish the fire.*

Groggy from the pill I had taken, I reached for the amour with my right hand. I could see nothing and, with my left hand, maneuvered around the foot of the bed until I reached the closed bedroom door. Coughing, choking, with my nose and eyes dripping, I had not thought about the possibility of an inferno on the other side of the door. I was running purely on fear and adrenaline. I yanked open the door. The flames were contained to my bedroom. I stumbled through the living room toward the kitchen. Clouds of smoke ballooned into the living room and a second deafening smoke alarm went off.

My brain was mush. I had no idea where the fire extinguisher was or even if I had one. I darted into the kitchen, filled a large pot with water, and ran back to the bedroom. Much of the water spilled on the carpet. I heaved the water at the rampant flames consuming the lampshade and the tall fake plant next to it.

The light bulb exploded with a loud, hard crack. I screamed and jumped backwards. Shards of glass shot into dozens of tiny pieces all over the floor. My heart was pounding out of my chest. I rushed back to the kitchen and returned to the bedroom with another pot of water and doused anything still smoking. No longer seeing flames, I tried to calm my racing heart and wipe my burning eyes. My throat felt raw. It was painful to swallow.

I turned on the ceiling fan and opened the bedroom window. Fresh air and moonlight streamed into the room, cutting through the smoky darkness. I stood in the doorway, assessing the damage. But where was Matt?

With the smoke detectors still shrieking, I grabbed a broom from the kitchen pantry and rammed the wooden handle into both shrill sounding ceiling alarms. Batteries and plastic pieces fell to the surrounding floor and the noise finally subsided. *All this commotion should have gotten Matt's attention.*

I looked in the office and living room to see if he was sleeping there. He was not. Rage replaced fear. I moved to the patio. He was not there either, but what I did notice was that the patio table was clean, reflecting the clouds in the moonlight, and the chairs were neatly tucked under each side of the table. This was not at all how I had left it. I tugged at the patio door to go out, but it was locked. I didn't remember doing that either.

I walked through the living room with an aching head, trying to reconstruct the events of the evening. That proved difficult. Was Matt's father at the house, or had I imagined that? I turned to inspect the kitchen. It was spotless. I closed my eyes, desperately wanting to believe that Matt was on a trip, and that I had some weird drug and alcohol induced nightmare. I wandered back into the bedroom and wondered why I would have lit candles if Matt was not home. He must have been home. I moved to the closet and was slapped in the face with reality, something even more unnerving than the fire damage. Matt's uniform and some of his clothes were missing.

What is going on? I grabbed my cell phone and called Matt, only to get his voicemail. "Matt, it's four in the morning and we had a fire at the house. Where are you? Call me."

Confused, I felt like the world was crashing down around me. I ran the gauntlet of emotions, moving from panic to rage to desperation. With my head pounding from the red wine that I had consumed over the course of the evening, I let the phone drop from my hand and I collapsed onto the floor. Reduced to a crumpled mess lying there feeling so alone, I sobbed hysterically.

It was light outside when the ring tone of my cell phone woke me. Disoriented, I had to think about why I was on the floor in the hallway rather than in my bed. But seeing the black soot on my hands, and smoke marks covering the walls and ceiling, I remembered.

I sat up. Matt was yelling into the phone before I had even said a word. "You left about four hysterical messages on my cell phone."

I couldn't believe my ears. "Yes," I said curtly. "I woke up with the bedroom on fire and you were nowhere to be found. I think that merits a little hysteria."

Matt said nothing.

I demanded answers. "What is going on and where are you?"

"Nothing is going on," Matt said in a nasty tone. "I didn't feel like fighting with you last night so I stayed at my dad's condo."

"You were here," I retorted. "And now all your airline clothes are gone."

Matt's voice was booming with anger. "I have a trip today so I just packed everything last night or were you so drunk you forgot."

Did he really think that I was that drunk or that stupid to believe his ridiculous excuses? That enraged me. "Why didn't you blow out the candles in the bedroom and why wouldn't you answer your phone."

Matt said nothing. The conversation was going nowhere, just like my marriage. Before ending the call I said to him, "We need to talk."

He reluctantly agreed. "Fine, Saturday when I return from my trip."

The phone went dead.

Hung over and completely unhinged, I wandered into the kitchen. *Thank God the coffee pot didn't burn up in the fire.* The more I thought about what had happened, the crazier it seemed. I saw my sooty reflection in the toaster and swiped at the black dust around my nose. The whole thing was surreal. One day I had a loving husband and the next not.

With a much needed cup of coffee in hand, I called the number on the back of my credit card. "I lost my card. What are the most recent charges on it?"

The man's response hit me like a bullet to the gut.

Completely spent, I collapsed onto the floor. A hollow feeling took hold. I was broken, possibly beyond repair. I cried and pleaded with a higher power to give me my old life back, to make everything the way it was before Londono's accusations, and before I discovered my husband's infidelity.

In a daze, I pushed myself up from the floor. There was something I needed to check on. I walked into the garage and saw different sizes of flat head screwdrivers and a few other tools strewn across Matt's work bench. I thought back to the afternoon I had returned home. It didn't look like that. I would have noticed. The top of the bench was usually bare. Matt was very good about keeping everything in its place.

I opened the door to my government car and reached in for my briefcase. After the tale I had told Matt, I was happy it was still there. But something was off. The handle was facing the seat back. I always had the front of the briefcase facing the windshield or the driver's side of the car, for easy access. I pulled my locked briefcase out into the light and saw scratches around the three number coded metal locks. Matt had tampered with it. I entered the three digit code and opened the briefcase. Inside, everything was as I had left it. The only documents contained inside were some bank statements. It appeared that Matt had given up on taking the so-called phone records, and decided to let them burn up in the fire.

I went back into the house and grabbed a bottle of vodka from the cupboard. How I wished this was a bad dream, but it wasn't. I wandered into the bedroom, popped a valium in my mouth, and washed it down with a long swig of vodka, then another.

A loud television commercial jolted me awake, or maybe it was the constant ringing of the phone. At one point, I thought I heard someone knocking on the door. It was probably Laurel. I ignored it. I didn't want to talk, think, or be alive. I couldn't tell if it was day or night thanks to the blackout curtains, nor did I care. I took another drink of vodka and went back to sleep.

PART THREE

ALL THAT REMAINS

CHAPTER 25

Present Day

I awake to the squeaking of my front door. I feel the sound in every nerve of my body. My heart races. Matt?

Then it all painfully comes rushing back. I lie motionless and stare at the comforter covering my face. I pull back the edge of the comforter to see if the bedroom door is open or closed. The empty vodka bottle rolls off the bed, almost in slow motion. It hits the floor with a loud thud.

Footsteps approach from the other side of the closed door and pause. Did Londono send one of his men to kill me, like he had done to my informants and Rosa?

I chuckle to myself. *Death would be the humane option.*

The bedroom door opens.

Paige gasps. "Oh, my god."

"What? Should I call 911?" Julie demands, poking her head in the door.

I peer out at them from under the comforter.

Paige stares at the glass shards, candle wax, and towels on the soot-covered carpet. "We came to make sure you weren't dead. What the hell happened in here?"

"I set the place on fire, now go away."

Paige yanks the comforter away from my chin. "No, we won't go away. I left you about ten messages in the last two days." Still scowling, she glares at the empty bottles of booze. "Why wouldn't you answer your phone? What's wrong with you?"

Julie plops on the foot of the bed. "You look like shit. When was the last time you washed your hair or took a shower, for that matter?"

I pull the comforter back up and roll onto my side. "Right after I put out the fire."

Paige, slightly more compassionate than Julie, squats down beside the bed, face to face with me, and holds up the empty vodka bottle. "This is not the answer. Get up and take a shower while we clean up around here. We're going out." Her words and stern gaze shut down my objections.

Julie grabs an empty potato chip bag off the bed, walks over to the window and pulls open the curtains. "And someplace that serves healthy food. I don't know how you stay so slim eating crap like this." She shakes the empty chip bag.

Because I had not seen daylight in two days, the pinkish glow of the early evening sky hurts my eyes. I squint.

Paige stands up and begins collecting trash from around the bed. "Get up. We'll wait for you in the living room."

Julie follows Paige out of the bedroom and closes the door.

A half hour later, I join my two friends in the kitchen. "Better?" I ask, referring to my appearance.

"Geez, Jenn," Julie says. "We thought maybe you confronted Matt, and he killed you."

Paige gazes over my shoulder at the burnt bedroom wall. "What happened?"

"The lampshade caught on fire."

"I can see that," Paige says. "What, you went out and left candles burning?"

"No, I passed out and Matt went out leaving the candles burning."

Julie chuckles. "What? Where were you?"

"Asleep."

Seated at the counter, Paige looks over at Julie and back at me. "Ok, start from the beginning."

"Matt cancelled his trip because his father was in town. His dad came over for dinner. Watching Matt act like everything was alright made me so angry that I said a few things to make him squirm. I told him that I had our phone records, and we were going to review them to charge Londono with impeding an investigation." I pause. "I guess he was afraid I would see the calls to his girlfriend."

Impatient, Julie waves her hand in circles. "Get to the part about the fire."

"I wanted to talk with Matt after he took his father home. I was nervous, so I took a valium. I lit candles and waited for him to return, but the pill knocked me out." I momentarily pause and begrudgingly confess the rest. "I also had a lot to drink during the course of the evening."

Paige disapprovingly shakes her head. "So, did you talk with him or didn't he come home?"

"Oh, he came home, cleaned everything up from dinner, then left. He just didn't extinguish the candles that I left burning next to the bed."

Paige takes a long pensive look at my pristine kitchen, stands up, and slowly walks through the living room, as if analyzing a crime scene. She lingers over the candles on the end tables, then moves to the cd player, where she pushes the power button. A loud David Bowie song plays. She pushes it again, turning it off. After gazing out at the patio for a long minute, she turns back to me with a very serious expression on her face. "You're telling me that he cleaned everything up, put things away, and extinguished the candles in these rooms, but he neglected to blow out candles in a dark bedroom near a lampshade?" She pauses. "I think he saw an opportunity."

"I agree," Julie says and walks back into the bedroom.

Paige and I follow and watch Julie assessing the damage. She then walks toward the master bathroom and stops outside the half-empty walk-in closet. Paige also peers into the closet, seeing mostly my clothes.

"Where's Matt clothes and pilot uniform?" Julie asks.
"He took it."

Julie looks over at Paige and raises her eyebrows. "I

hate to sound grim and suspicious, but it sure seems like the guy wanted you dead. He saw how easy a fire could occur and how he could just walk away unscathed."

I touch a picture of me and Matt and stare at the soot on my finger. "Looking back, I now see all the warnings signs that I missed. But for him to want to harm me?"

"I'm sorry," Julie replies, "But think about it. You have lots of assets and a husband who doesn't have the balls to tell you that he wants a divorce. So, what does he do? He takes his uniforms and clothes to his dad's, so if a fire destroys the house and kills you in the process, he won't be terribly inconvenienced."

I wrap my arms around my middle. "I know, but..."

"No, listen to me," Paige says with her eyes boring into mine. "I'm serious. If you and I were hearing this from a witness or defendant, we would be telling that person that this was an attempted murder. The only difference is that it's Matt we're talking about."

I feel the life I had quickly shifting, fading, and disappearing. With my hands covering my eyes, I mournfully say, "You're right. He's the beneficiary on my Thrift Savings Plan, retirement plan, government life insurance, and everything else."

Paige gingerly takes my arm and leads me back into the kitchen. Again seated at the counter, she says, "I don't think we know this guy at all, and I'm telling you as a friend that Matt's actions are scaring me. I don't think you should be alone with him from this point on."

I feel a tightness in my chest. "I know. I now see what he's capable of. Or at the very least that he doesn't care about what happens to me." I shake my head. "I feel ridiculous. I'm a trained investigator. I got so wrapped up with the Londono thing that I didn't see this coming."

"You trusted him," Paige says.

"So, is he at his parent's condo or on a trip?" Julie asks.

I half laugh as a tear streaks down my cheek. "Actually, he's in a three hundred and fifty dollar room at the Marriott Beachfront hotel with his girlfriend."

Paige and Julie exchange shocked expressions.

"Yep, I checked with the credit card company. He checked in at twelve o'clock last night."

Julie shakes her head. "Jenn, you have to end this now."

CHAPTER 26

Before Matt was to arrive home on Saturday, I needed to copy all the documents he would be taking with him in the divorce. Julie asked Anne, Kim, and Karen to help us, and Paige told Laurel what was going on. All agreed to assist with what they called the sending-Matt-packing event.

On the way home from work, I stopped at the grocery store to pick up beer, wine, and snacks. Still reeling from the pain of Matt's betrayal, I lost all interest in cooking. Pizza delivery will have to suffice for dinner.

Nowadays, it's all I can do to hold it together at the office. But when I'm alone in the car on the drive to or from work, the tears flow nonstop.

Just past six o'clock, I lean back in my ergonomic office chair and watch my friends diligently sort through my personal documents, separating out anything of Matt's that may be important to me at a later date.

"The attorney couldn't believe that Matt signed away all rights to both properties," I tell the women.

"I don't mean to sound like Debbie Downer," Julie says. "But could he have done that because he had planned on killing you all along?"

Paige flips through the file she has in her hands, and glances at the other women in the room. "Don't apologize. You just said what the rest of us were thinking."

It's difficult for me to pack up Matt's belongings. I look at our wedding picture on the desk and remember how Matt whispered in my ear as we were being photographed. I even recall his words. "This is the best day of my life."

That was over seven years ago. Now, heart broken, I move from room to room, reflecting on happier times. What had happened? Did I drive him into the arms of another woman because of my fears and overprotective behavior regarding the cartel?

"When are you telling Matt that you know about the chic?" Kim, a tall, slim blonde dance instructor, asks as she pulls files from a desk drawer.

"Tomorrow when he returns from his trip," I reply. "The records will be copied, the locks changed, and his stuff will be out of the house. I want to surprise him just like he surprised me."

Karen, a petite, blonde ICU nurse, hugs me and picks up two boxes of documents. "To expedite the process, Kim and I are going to copy these over at our houses. We should be back in about an hour."

I help the two of them carry boxes out to their cars. When I return to the office, it looks like the four remaining women have just been told that their best friend died.

"Okay, spill it," I say, surprised by the flat unemotional tone of my voice.

Julie, acting as the spokesperson for the group, says, "We found something interesting we want you to see."

I scan their concerned faces. "Interesting good or interesting bad?"

Julie holds up a zip-lock bag full of cash. I take the baggy from Julie and inspect it with the fervor of a DEA agent who has just been handed a package of white powder.

The women could see that I didn't know about the money, so Laurel set the scene. "It was hidden in one of those manila envelopes marked 'old crew reports'."

"Did you count it?" I ask, handing the money to Paige.

"Yep," Julie replies. "It's just short of ten thousand dollars."

"My best guess is Londono." I say, as I watch Paige fan the money out across the top of the desk and snap pictures of it with her cell phone.

"If not the drug guy, where else would he have gotten

it?" Anne asks.

Mentally exhausted, I shrug. "When I analyzed our bank records I noticed a lot of ATM withdrawals. Matt was gradually siphoning money out of our joint account, but not that much. So, I have no idea, and I am quickly realizing that there is way too much that I don't know."

"I'll bet it was Matt who tripped the alarm on New Year's Eve," Anne says. "Didn't you tell him that you were staying with Julie?"

Paige returns the cash to the zip-lock bag and hands it back to me.

"Maybe he was out with that girl, ran short of funds, and stopped by to pick up a few extra bucks," Laurel adds, tossing a stack of folders into an empty box. "They were probably out at that new casino near here."

Julie laugh-snorts. "I'm sorry, Jenn, she's right. With every turn, the plot thickens and we discover another one of Matt's dirty secrets, women and hidden funds. This whole thing is looking more and more like a Lifetime movie."

"Except these bizarre events are happening to me," I reply.

Laurel snickers. "I would check to make sure he's not married to another woman."

"Or women," Anne adds. "What if he also has a gambling problem, and that's where the money came from? He won it."

"I hope that's the case," Paige says, looking at me. "I hate Matt for what he's done, but if we find any connection between him and Londono, that elevates him to a whole new level of depravity."

I drop the zip-lock bag of cash onto the desk and push it over to Paige as if it were a dead mouse I didn't want to handle. "Could you put that in the gun safe at your house? For now, I think it's best to keep it out of Matt's reach. It may be leverage I can use later."

"Maybe even evidence," Anne and Laurel say, in

unison, before going back to the bedroom to finish packing Matt's clothes.

I rest my head on the desk while Julie continues looking through a stack of financial documents. I inhale deeply, sit up straight, and go back to putting credit card statements in sequential order for Julie to copy.

Within minutes, I find an item that had given me pause months earlier. "This statement lists a three hundred and sixty-five dollar purchase and a reversal of the item. Matt said he charged the room for his co-pilot, who didn't have a credit card on him. I'll bet that was another lie."

Julie stops what she's doing. "Who doesn't carry a credit card on them nowadays?"

I call the number on the statement and chat with a representative, while Julie sits anxiously waiting to hear the results. I thank the representative and end the call. Julie can tell from the bleak look on my face that it isn't good. "What now?"

"I'm so stupid. I thought it strange, but once again I trusted Matt. He charged a room at Hawk's Cay Resort in Key Largo and then backed it off our credit card by paying cash for the room when he arrived."

"I take it that you weren't with him at the resort?" Julie replies, looking over my shoulder at the statement.

"No, I wasn't," I mumble. "That was our seventh wedding anniversary."

Paige enters the office and sees the sad expression on my face. She looks to Julie for answers. "What's up?"

"She uncovered another one of Matt's lies that we can add to his never ending list," Julie replies.

Paige shakes her head. "What, more money?"

"No," Julie says. "This is a vacation with the girlfriend in the Keys on Jennifer and Matt's wedding anniversary."

Carrying two full boxes of Matt's clothes, to be sealed up and tossed into the garage, Laurel and Anne walk in on the tail end of the conversation and watch as my anger gives way to hatred toward the man I thought I knew. "Matt showed me his schedule, or the one he obviously doctored up for me. He said he had to work that weekend. I was willing to travel with him for our anniversary, but he said he couldn't do that to me, too many legs to the trip. Now, I know why."

Anne drops the box of clothes she is holding. "Oh my God, this guy is unbelievable. He probably told his girlfriend he couldn't see her that weekend because it was your anniversary and she forced the issue, making him choose between you or her. He is truly a pig."

At the top of the box Anne was holding, I spot Matt's tropical Tommy Bahama shirt. Matt, the handsome charming man who made me laugh and quiver with pleasure, was a charlatan. I grab the shirt from the box. "This was my anniversary gift to Matt." Taking a Sharpie highlighter from the desk, I run the tip of the marker up and down the back of the shirt, until a thick yellow line can be seen.

Laughing, Julie cries out, "You go, girl."

I put the cap on the marker and hand the shirt back to Anne. "Can you fold this so he won't notice my artwork right away? I hope Matt wears the shirt in public and someone tells him that he has a yellow steak down his back."

I move around the room rifling through the stacks of documents on the floor, desk, and sofa.

"What are you looking for?" Julie asks.

"These." I hold up the statements from Matt's previous cell phone company and quickly review each one.

The women watch in silence until they see me shaking my head. "What is it?" Paige asks.

"As you all discovered, for tax purposes, I keep everything during the year." I hold up pages from an invoice. "Her phone number is on the August statement. It didn't start two months ago. He's been seeing the tramp most of this year. I'll bet I find her number on last year's statements as well."

Laurel takes some statements from my hand. "Here, I found another one with an Atlanta prefix. Is this her number?"

I look at the phone number Laurel is pointing at. "No, her number ends in 2324. I don't know whose number that is."

Anne looks over Laurel's shoulder. "There are some other calls here to Atlanta. It looks like he's been seeing a few flight attendants."

***

Two hours later, after we finish packing his stuff and copying records, we relax on the patio with pizza and beer.

Julie holds up her Corona Light. "Ladies, here's to a job well done. After everything we uncovered tonight, I hope that message Jennifer left for Matt on their anniversary weekend telling him about an alienation of affection lawsuit ruined his romantic holiday."

"Here, here," the women cheer.

I stare up at the night sky and then back to the group. "I don't know why, but I always thought men cheated only because they were unhappy and not getting enough sex at home or the relationship lacked passion. The articles I'm now reading say that's just one of many reasons, and most have nothing to do with the woman, and everything to do with the man. He's insecure, immature, selfish, or lacking a moral code.

Anne rubs my arm. "Or has opportunity and is doing it because he can like Matt."

"I never saw myself in this situation. This has been a very humbling experience. I watch all those Lifetime movies and always wonder how it is that the wives don't see what's happening. Now I understand it because I am one of those women."

Laurel gently pats my back. "How could you have known? We've all spent a lot of time with the two of you and none of us suspected this. Matt is very good at pretending that he is the perfect loving, attentive husband."

"A Doctor Jekyll Mister Hyde personality," Anne adds.

Julie raises her beer and makes a toast. "Yes, this situation sucks, but you have us, so here's to good friends and moving forward."

Kim darts into the house and returns with a piece of paper. "Last, but not least, let's run down this checklist of things you needed to do, such as changing the utilities over to your name and opening a new bank account."

"Check," I reply.

"Has your realtor scheduled a locksmith for the Atlanta house?" Julie asks.

"Tomorrow," I say, walking around the table and gathering up empty bottles.

At the close of the evening, I hug each of the women and walk them to the front door. "Thank you all for everything."

"Stay at my place," Paige suggests. "We can't be sure that Matt is actually on a trip?"

"Yes, he may come back to finish what he started, like another fire," Anne suggests.

CHAPTER 27

Early Saturday morning, Robin calls. "Hey, I'm at your house with the locksmith. I heard a telephone ringing and located a phone in the master bedroom tucked under the bed."

"You found a phone in our bedroom?"

"Yes, it was hidden, out of sight," Robin replies in her thick southern drawl. "I thought you told me that you didn't have telephone service at this house."

"It sounds like we do," I snicker, thinking of Matt's endless deceptions.

Robin laughs. "Yes, ma'am, and my friend at the phone company said the account is in Matt's name."

"He's just full of surprises."

"You want me to snoop around the house and see what else I might find, or are you all surprised out?"

"Definitely snoop. And Robin? Feel free to make lots of long-distance calls from that phone. Don't just think local, think international calls."

"You got it. I'll call you again before locking the house back up."

I smell the aroma of coffee, and go downstairs where Paige is seated at her kitchen table reading the morning paper. She has cereal and English muffins on the counter.

When her two adorable children see me, they tear themselves away from cartoons to ask me if I will spend another night with them.

"I would love to, but I won't know about that until later this afternoon or this evening," I tell them."

"Oh, please, try, try," Hannah pleads.

"Okay, let Jenn and I talk," Paige says, and the two scamper back to their cartoons.

Paige gets up and pours me a cup of coffee. "I heard

your phone. Is everything okay?"

"While changing locks at the Atlanta house, Robin found a telephone, and the account is in Matt's name." I pour cream in my coffee and take a long sip. "I have Robin looking around to see what else he may be hiding."

No sooner do I finish my sentence when Robin calls. "If you were surprised about the phone connectivity, you had better be sitting down for this next bit of news."

"Go ahead."

"There's quite a bit of women's clothing in one of the guest bedrooms," Robin comments. "Also, there are a few articles of men's clothing at the other end of that closet. If some pilot is renting that bedroom, do you think those clothes could belong to his wife? Maybe she flies to Atlanta to spend time with her husband, like what you were doing before you discovered that Matt had a little something on the side."

"No, I don't think that's the situation. With everything I've discovered about Matt, I'll bet he has the woman he is seeing living in our house, especially since she has an Atlanta phone number, and Matt has been spending so much time up there, supposedly fixing up the house. I can resolve this easily enough. I'll call you back as soon as I speak to the pilot who's renting that room."

I scroll through a list of contacts on my phone until I find the name I'm looking for. I touch the number on the screen and wait. My call is answered on the first ring.

"Jason? This is Jennifer Weber."

"How are you, Jennifer?" the man politely asks.

"Fine," I lie. "We're having a plumbing issue upstairs and may need to move you and your wife's clothes into one of the other bedrooms temporarily until the work is complete."

"That's fine with me. As I recall, I only have a hoody and a couple of jeans in the closet. You'll have to talk to Matt or that flight attendant about all those other items."

"Oh, I thought all the clothes in that closet belonged

to you and your wife."

"Not at all. Matt told me that one of the flight attendants he works with is in the process of moving and he's helping her out by keeping some of her things at the house until she gets settled. I really wasn't using the closet space, so her belongings ended up in my room."

"Weren't you worried that you would have a lot of explaining to do if your wife came to visit and saw another woman's clothes in your room? I know something like that would upset me."

Jason chuckles. "Matt said there would be hell to pay if he put them in your bedroom. I told my wife what was going on, and she had no problem with it. She also went back to school to get her Master's Degree and has no time for vacation or even weekend jaunts, so there was no problem with storing things in my room."

I thank the pilot for his time and call Robin. "I spoke with the pilot who is renting that room and guess what?"

"Those are not his wife's clothes," Robin replies. "I saw that one coming a mile away."

"Yep, Matt said the clothes belong to a flight attendant who is moving."

"Right," Robin adds sarcastically, "Moving into your house."

"Isn't that the truth? So, would you be kind enough to toss those clothes in the trash for me?"

"I'll put the clothes in the trash can and on the curb for tomorrow's pickup."

Seated at the table listening to the conversation, Paige says, "Write a book so other wives will know what to look out for."

I hold up my phone. "Oh, Matt left me a message."

I play back his message on speaker so Paige can hear. "Hi, I'm in between flights, and I need to talk to you about a message I received from your prosecutor. Call me when you get this. Oh, and I'll be home around four o'clock." His tone is pleasant, and it reminded me of the loving, easy-going man I thought I knew. Before ending his message, he even mentions meeting some place for drinks.

I smile at Paige. "I know the perfect spot to meet him."

"You do know that I'm not going to let you meet him alone, even out in public. Don't toy with him again. You saw what he did the last time."

"Don't worry." I touch his number on my phone.

"Hello," Matt says cheerfully. "Thank you for getting back to me straight away. How are you doing?"

"I'm fine," I casually reply, putting him on speaker. "What's up?"

"As I said in my message, I received a call from Robert Mullaney. He wants to meet with me. This has me rather concerned. Can you give me a heads up on what he wants to discuss with me before I call him back?"

"Oh sure," I say, and think, *I'll help you just like you have been there for me during the last few months...not.* "It's about those calls we were receiving."

Paige closes her eyes and shakes her head.

I wink at her. "Robert subpoenaed our phone records and saw that some calls you received had pinged off of a Miami cell phone tower."

"Maybe one of my pilot friends called me from there. Will you be attending this meeting?"

"I wasn't invited, but you'll do fine." Then I said to myself. *Just lie like you have been and maybe we can charge you with providing false information.*

"Alright, I have to go. They're almost finished with the boarding process. Do you want to meet somewhere so we can talk more about this and other things?"

"How about the Cat's Fiddle?"

"Sounds good. I'll call you when I get in."

I hang up and see a disturbed look on Paige's face. "I don't understand why you want to meet with him at all. Tell him what you know over the phone or send him a text message about where to find his belongings. That's way more than he deserves."

"I want him to look me in the face and tell me why he did it. And I want to do this at the English pub where we had our wedding reception."

Paige frowns. "Even if you talk with him, you may not learn anything more than you already know. He's been lying for who knows how long. Maybe he's not capable of telling the truth, or maybe he doesn't even know what the truth is anymore."

I nod in agreement. "You left out dangerous."

Paige sighs. "Yes, and he's very dangerous."

An unpleasant feeling slithers through me and I reflect on the night of the fire.

CHAPTER 28

I go with Paige to her children's karate class. While watching the kids, I overhear the woman sitting next to us tell someone on the phone how her husband was supposed to be home from golf in time to take their son to karate. She complains that her husband never does what he says he'll do. That gets me to thinking. Is Matt really on a trip or is he staying at his parent's condo with his girlfriend.

After the class, we pick up some food for the kids and take them home. I grab my car keys and tell Paige that I'm going to see if Matt's car is in the airport employee lot, and that I'll return in a few hours.

I jump in my car and head south to the airport. I drive up and down the road adjacent to the airport employee parking lot, and spot several gray cars, none of them Matt's.

Out of the corner of my eye, I see something in my rearview mirror. A car is rapidly approaching from behind. Due to the glare of the sun and a dirty rear windshield, I can't make out the make or color of the car rapidly bearing down on me. It's dark like Matt's car. I tense up, remembering what Julie had said about Matt. "He's driving like a bat out of hell."

When I look up again, he's on my tail, so close that I can't see the front of his car. A horn loudly blares. I flinch. Is it Matt? I can't tell. I again look in the rearview mirror. Wrong move. I accidentally swerve off the single lane road and stomp on the brakes. The black Volvo speeds past. My car skids to a stop in a swirl of dirt and gravel. Surrounded by dust, I exhale all the nervous tension from my lungs, and call Paige. "It looks like you were right about us not knowing if Matt is really away on a trip. I'm at the airport and I am certain that his car is not here."

"Are you on your way back?"

"I have two more stops, then I'll be back."

Paige sighs. "Be careful and if you spot him, do not confront him. I spoke with Julie. She's going to take you to meet Matt this evening and will wait for you at that location. I'll park out on the street in front of your house. This may be a trick where he wants you waiting for him at that pub, while he goes in the house and gets whatever he didn't take with him the first time."

"Now that you mention it, I wonder why he didn't take the cash the night of the fire."

"Who knows and who cares. Maybe he was frazzled and forgot about it. After all, this was probably his first attempted murder."

"Ha ha. See you in a bit." After catching Matt in so many lies, all I felt was betrayal. My only satisfaction is knowing how shocked he'll be when he realizes that I removed him from the credit cards, only left ten dollars in our joint bank account, and changed the locks on both the Atlanta and Florida homes.

I regain my composure and head for the beachfront Marriott where Matt and his girlfriend stayed on the night of the fire. I peruse the parking lot. His car is not there.

On the way back to Paige's house, I cautiously drive around the parking lot of his parents' condo. Just hours away from ending this charade, I didn't want Matt to see my car and get spooked. I see his parents' parking space in front of the building. It's empty. I cautiously zip out of the development, keeping my eyes open for Matt's car, fearing that he and the whore are out for the afternoon and may return any minute.

On the drive back to Paige's, I receive a text from Matt. *Flight lands at 4. Can meet you at the pub at 5.*

I scoff at the text and wonder. *Is this guy even capable of telling the truth?*

Arriving back at Paige's house, I tell her where I

went. "I don't think he's been to our house because if he had been he would have asked about the locks."

"You said the girlfriend has Florida tags on her car. I wonder if they are staying with friends or her family." Paige says. "We can have Karen and Kim also park outside the pub, and have the two of them follow him to see where he goes after you and Julie leave."

"After I confront him, I don't care where he goes as long as it's not to my house."

"Wrong," Paige says. "You need to get as much info on him and her until he signs the settlement agreement."

***

As planned, at four in the afternoon, I drive over to my house and park in the garage. Paige parks down the street with a view of the front of the house, while Laurel and Anne sit on Laurel's patio, keeping an eye on the back of the house.

I jump into the passenger seat of Julie's car.

"Congratulations on passing the polygraph. That must be a relief." Julie says, backing out of my driveway.

I stare out the window. "Yep, now let's hope this works out as well."

The plan was for Julie to transport me to and from the pub, where I was meeting up with Matt, and for her to remain in the parking lot watching as events unfold to make sure Matt does not try anything funny.

Julie pulls into the rather empty parking lot of the British pub where Matt and I had our wedding reception just seven years earlier. Matt's car is parked near the front door of the bar.

"Of all places, I can't believe you asked him to meet you here."

I shrug. "It's where we celebrated a beginning and

now where I tell him it's the end." I jump out of the car.

"I'll be watching," Julie calls out through the open window.

I walk into the pub. It takes my eyes a minute to adjust from bright light to the dimly lit bar atmosphere. I spot Matt sitting at the bar, handsome as ever in his faded jeans and IZOD shirt. My heart ferociously pounds, then anger sets in. He had told me that he was on a trip, yet here he was, not in uniform. Should I question him about it, and make him spin a yarn you could knit a king size blanket with? No, I didn't want to hear any more of his lies.

I nervously sit next to him and ask the barmaid for a chardonnay.

"Hello," he says pleasantly, acting as if nothing is wrong or has happened. He doesn't kiss me or run his hand up and down my back as he normally would. Nope, he's testing the water. Before any of that, he's wanting to see how mad I am, and if I've forgiven him as I, so stupidly, had done so many times in the past.

My mind flashes back to the time he was more than an hour late picking me up from the repair shop where I had dropped off my car. It's funny how you recall the most inane things in the worst moments of your life. That day, too, he hadn't answered his cell phone when I called. I now know that his story about his flight being late and missing the employee bus was a lie. He was with another woman.

Matt, the opportunistic charmer, smiles and asks the barmaid for a refill on his gin and tonic before starting our conversation off with small talk. "Are you working out of the DEA offices down the street from here?"

The barmaid returns with the drinks, glances at my solemn expression, and returns to a group of patrons at the other end of the bar.

I take two big gulps of the wine, and rather than answering his question, I casually say, "Let's talk about you. Were you with Olivia at Embassy Suites or did you take her someplace nicer like the Marriott Beach Resort?"

A frown sinks into his forehead. In an attempt to mask his shock, Matt growls, "What are you talking about?"

I stare directly into his denim blue eyes, and with tears streaming down my face, say, "I'm talking about Liv Ogden, the flight attendant who resides at 1010 Waycross Avenue, Atlanta, Georgia, and frequently at my new home in Newnan."

Matt jumps up as if he's going to bolt for the door.

His actions are so exaggerated that it catches the attention of the observant barmaid, who looks prepared to run out to the parking lot and jot down his license plate number if he were to stiff her on the tab.

Matt stops just short of the door and sits down in a corner booth, out of view from the barmaid and the other patrons. He places his face in his hands, and with his shoulders heaving, it appears that he's crying.

The barmaid, who is keeping an eye on Matt, slowly approaches me and points at my empty glass. "I'll get you another one, unless you want something stronger."

I offer her a thin smile. "Wine is fine."

She fills my glass to the brim, and we both watch as Matt tries to get his emotions in check. He then motions for me to join him.

The barmaid and I exchange somber looks.

"Let me know if you need anything," she says.

I walk over to Matt's table. "I'm not going to make a scene. I just want to know why you did it."

"I don't know," he replies. "One thing just led to another."

I sit down across from him. "Do you love her?"

He stares deep into my eyes. "No, she's just fun, that's all."

With all my heart, I wanted to believe him. Then, I remember the lies. "All those hang-up calls? That was her, not some telemarketer or manic drug dealer stalking us, wasn't it?"

Matt wipes tears from his face. "Yes, she gets very insecure when I'm at home with you."

His words enrage me. "Insecure because you told her you were going to divorce me and it wasn't happening as quickly as she wanted?"

"No, No I told her I wasn't going to get a divorce."

"Oh, so you were going to sneak around with her behind my back, make a fool of me, and just let me believe that someone wanted to kill me?"

Matt reaches for my hand. "I'm so sorry. It was just easier than telling you about her."

Furious, I pull my hand away. "What about just ending it? Why didn't you put a stop to everything that made it look like our lives were in danger?"

"Please, it's over with her. I'll tell her I don't want to see her again."

"You should have done that a long time ago," I reply. "You hurt me so deeply. You humiliated me, and most of all I can never trust you again."

Matt stares at a spot on the table top and shakes his head in agreement. "I know. I'm stupid. I'm sorry."

I look at Matt's cell phone lying on the table and shove it toward him. "Okay, then call her. Tell her it's over."

I hadn't changed my mind about divorce. I just wanted to cause the whore some grief, much like she had done to me.

Matt picks up the phone and pushes a button. *Nice, he has her on speed dial.* I hear a woman answer. "I'm here with Jennifer. She knows everything, so it's over between us." I hear the woman respond, but can't tell what she is saying. Matt hangs up and puts the phone back on the table.

Because I had become acutely aware of how cunning he could be, I grab the phone up to see who he had really called. I didn't expect what came next. The caller id displays the name Gary. My mouth drops open. I glare across the table.

"I can explain."

My heart is thumping and my mouth is dry. "All those calls were from her."

Matt reaches out to touch my cheek. "I was going to tell you."

I turn my head to avoid his touch. "You are unbelievable. I loved you so much. I used to think that you were the best person in this world. Remember when I would tell you that I aspired to be like you?"

It pained Matt to hear those words. He tries to speak, but he's so choked up that the words do not come out.

"I can't be married to you anymore," I say, wiping the tears from my cheeks. "You've shown me that our marriage means nothing to you. I have an attorney and an appointment for us at nine o'clock Monday morning."

I push the attorney's card across the table to Matt. "Please do the right thing *for once* and be there. Your belongings are boxed up on the front porch."

He tries to grab my hand as I get up to leave. "Please, I love you. Don't do this."

"I didn't do this," I firmly reply. "You did."

Quickly exiting the pub, I jump into Julie's car. We travel in silence for a few miles until she finally asks, "Did you get your questions answered?"

"No," I reply. "No answers that are going to change anything."

CHAPTER 29

"Jenn, let's go inside," Julie says.

I look around and realize that we're parked in my driveway. Paige, who had been watching the front of the house, in case Matt were to send someone over to get his cash hoard, pulls her car up beside Julie.

"How you doing?" Paige asks.

"Not good," I say. "My dream of happily ever after didn't just fade away. It was ripped from my hands and stomped on right before my eyes."

Paige and Julie exchange quizzical glances.

Inside, I pour the three of us some wine and give them the short version of what transpired in the bar. "It's finally over. I should be happy."

"Give it time," Julie says.

After experiencing so much pain, fear, and grief, my brain just switched off. "I'm going to bed."

The pair watch me with expressions of unease.

As I close the bedroom door, I hear Julie tell Paige that her daughter is with her ex-husband for the weekend. "So, I'll spend the night here just in case, Matt...."

"Ah yes, Matt." I lay down, touch his empty side of the bed, and cry myself to sleep.

I awake to a loud sound. The sun is out and someone is knocking on the patio door. I sit straight up in bed. *Matt?* I listen and hear women's voices. I look at my phone. I have three messages. I assume most of them are from Matt. *Now you know how it feels to have your calls go unanswered.*

It's Sunday morning. I wander into the kitchen. Laurel and Anne hold up bottles of champagne and orange juice.

"Paige is on her way over with breakfast muffins," Julie announces in a cheerful tone.

"Perfect," Laurel replies, uncorking a bottle. "What about Kim and Karen?"

POP. I flinch at the sound. Compassionately, the women gaze at me for a long moment. Anne finally turns away and pulls champagne glasses from the cupboard.

I hear the front door squeak open. I turn quickly, optimistically. My heart bolts. *Matt?*

I wait and watch.

Paige strolls into the kitchen carrying two bags of muffins.

Julie sees my reaction. "I unlocked the front door in case we were on the patio and couldn't hear her knocking."

I stand there wondering. What is it that I'm hoping for? Do I want Matt to charge in, tell me that he'll do anything to right his wrongs, and beg me to take him back? Absolutely. But trust has been broken, and regardless of how much I want the life I once had, it can never be.

Dazed, I hear my friends chatting. I have no idea what they're talking about. My mind is elsewhere. It's all just white noise, like having the television or radio on in the background. I watch them moving about, preparing a lovely brunch. Life is going on around me. I'm just an onlooker, a mere bystander.

Paige draws me back into reality by handing me a note from Matt. "I found it wedged in the front door."

"So, he was here," Julie says.

Paige hands Julie the bags of food. "He must've seen your car in the driveway and decided not to knock or use his key."

"And he wouldn't," I reply. "Matt knows that Julie is a gun carrying agent, and being the coward he is, he didn't want to take a chance on her popping a cap in his ass."

I silently read the note. It was much like the phone messages he had left. He apologizes and writes all the right things. However, after everything he has done over the last two months, nothing can deter me from divorce. These are words I have to keep telling myself.

Around one o'clock, Kim and Karen arrive with everything to make the perfect Bloody Mary. Laurel leaves for a while and returns with an Italian salad, and a fabulous charcuterie board. The food, drink, and company are just what I needed. We hang out in and around the pool until evening.

I don't hear anything more from Matt. I assure my friends that I'll be fine, and I decline all offers to spend the night elsewhere.

After everything is cleaned up, locked up, and the women leave, I try to come to terms with my new life as a divorcee.

***

I don't set my alarm to go off the next morning. I hope to sleep in until my attorney calls to deliver good news.

Days earlier, I had informed both Moore and Szish that I would be meeting with my divorce attorney on Monday and would not be coming to work. They both wished me the best and told me to call if I needed anything. I felt guilty about taking a page from Matt's playbook, and lying about the meeting that I would not be attending, but I also knew that I would be worthless sitting at the office waiting to hear the outcome from the attorney.

The clock on the stove displays the time as nine o'clock. I'm a bundle of nerves pacing around the house. My mind is racing. Every time the phone rings, I get butterflies in my stomach. The calls are from Kim, Karen, Julie, and Anne.

Laurel stops over to check on me. With a cup of coffee in hand, I say, "I hope my attorney leaves Matt sitting in the reception area for a good long time. I want him to worry about what is going on and where I am. I want Matt to experience a little of what I have been going through, hoping that the situation is not as bad as it seems and that things will go back to normal, only to have those dreams crushed."

After Laurel leaves, the hours pass slowly. I imagine Matt sitting at the attorney's desk, fuming over the loss of his Florida and Atlanta homes. With every computer game I play and each email I send, I glance at the time display on the bottom right of the computer monitor.

At ten thirty, I check my cell phone to make sure it's not turned to the silent mode. Next, I busy myself with housecleaning. At eleven o'clock, I start pacing again. Finally, I call Paige. "I've heard nothing. What could be taking so long?"

"These things take time," she replies.

"Maybe I asked for too much because I'm hurt and angry."

Paige snickers. "What did you ask for?"

"Everything," I reply. Then my phone beeps, indicating I have another call. I look at the number on the screen. "That's my attorney. I'll call you back."

"Tell me something good," I say.

"Matt agreed to everything you requested and signed it all over to you. How's that?"

I exhale loudly. "That's wonderful."

"I'll file the signed document with the court. My secretary will send you a copy and notify you when it's final."

"Thank you so much," I say, and hang up the phone. *I should be ecstatic.* Instead, tears run down my face as I walk through the house, reliving memories of good times I had with the man I thought I was going to spend the rest of my life with. *He didn't even put up a fight. The man who constantly told me how much he loved me and how he couldn't live without me didn't offer to go to marriage counseling or sex addiction treatment. Nothing.*

I call Paige back. "The good news is that Matt agreed

to everything. I should be happy, but I'm not.

Paige meets me for lunch and smiles across the table at me. "I don't know if anyone told you, but Rosa's ex-husband provided Mullaney with a handwritten letter from Rosa. The letter detailed Londono's drug trafficking operation, and I'm talking about dates, locations, and amounts. She explained that the fifteen kilos of cocaine were Londono's and claimed that if she was found dead, it was at the hands of Londono."

"Will the ex-husband testify to that?"

"Yes, as will Theo Rojas," Paige replies, finishing her salad. "We also have a hand writing expert reviewing the document. And Mullaney has me and Ryan checking Rosa's account of shipments received against DEA surveillance reports we have on the couriers. He has your replacement looking into at all deposits or to see if any large purchases were made with cash around the dates the shipments came in."

"Did Rojas say anything about the deaths of my informants?"

"Yes. Londono had someone working in Rafael Morales' restaurant who told him that something was up. And as for Orlando Perez, well, it was like Steve suggested. Orlando told Londono that we had approached him, and that he would disappear for $20,000. Londono had his men get rid of him for free."

"Good, it's all coming together."

Paige nods. "Mullaney interviewed Rosa's mother, and she told him that Rosa opened a bank account for her, but she didn't know how much money was in it. She authorized her daughter to make deposits and withdrawals from that account and claimed that Rosa handled everything online, so she didn't know very much. Her story was that she just assumed any deposits were occasional bonuses Rosa received from her work and any withdrawals would be incidentals for the kids. She also said that Rosa had instructed her to close the account in the event of her death."

In between bites of salad, I smirk. "We all know that's bullshit, but the combination of her story and her age will play on the heartstrings of the jury and most likely keep her out of jail. That was probably why Rosa set it up that way."

"Mullaney's not going to file charges against her. And the best news, aside from yours, is that with all this new information, Mullaney has filed a superseding indictment of RICO conspiracy and murder. That will put Londono away for life."

After lunch, I head home. On the drive, I call Mullaney. "Robert, how about a press release stating that in the back yard of Theo Rojas' house, Londono's second in command, DEA dug up and seized cash which was the equivalent to the amount Londono would have received for the sale of fifteen kilos of cocaine on the open market?"

"Yes, Ms. Weber," Mullaney replies sarcastically. "I have already taken care of that and my office will be issuing a press release later today that will hopefully remove the proverbial target from yours and Steve's backs, just in case that still exists."

I hang up and dial the number on the back of my credit card. "Yes hello, as the primary card holder, I would like to have my husband, Matt, removed from the account, effective immediately."

CHAPTER 30

The Newnan house was sold within weeks of being on the market, and that was over a month ago. Time seems to pass so slowly when you're merely plodding along through life Three months have passed since my divorce. Still, I find it hard to get used to walking into a dark, empty house every night.

Tonight, as usual, I enter the house and my cat, Weezer, is there to greet me. Instead of rolling around like he used to, he seems to sense my sadness and just follows me into the kitchen. I feed him, grab a glass of wine, and call Paige.

"You'll get used to being single," she says. "I didn't have it so hard because I have the kids and a nanny."

I take a sip of wine and wander out to the patio. "Can I borrow them?"

"Any time you like."

"A flight attendant friend told me that Matt has moved to Atlanta."

"I would think that is good news," Paige says. "Unlike your friends with children, you won't see him anywhere or have to deal with him on a regular basis."

I dip my toes in the tepid pool water. "Yeah, it would hurt to run into him with another woman. After seven years of what I thought was a blissful marriage, I realize that the healing process is not going to be easy, and that it's going to take time to recover and move on with my life. Thanks for listening. I'll talk to you tomorrow."

To help me forget, I immerse myself in work. I'm back in the HIDTA task force and working on a new drug case. Londono was charged with everything under the sun and sentenced to twenty years in prison.

I find it relatively easy to make it through the busy workday without feeling as if I want to curl up into a ball and cry. The nights are more difficult. Wandering around an empty house and drudging up old memories often leaves me depressed. To make it through, I sometimes pretend that Matt is just away on a trip, like before the divorce.

Karen thinks it's time that I get back into the single lifestyle. So, on this particular Friday night, my friends arrange for a girl's night out at the beach.

I sit at a high-top table, covered with exotic fruity drinks at Lulu's Bait Shack on Ft. Lauderdale Beach, with the six of my closest females friends.

Laughing and admiring a breathtaking view overlooking the Atlantic Ocean, Anne tells the waitress, "Keep the drinks coming," which the waitress does.

To memorialize the evening, in the noisy crowded environment, we let the bar photographer take pictures of us making funny faces for the camera.

Swaying to the loud music, Karen yells out, "This place is great. We should come here more often."

"Yeah," Kim says, slurring her words. "Why don't we ever come out here?"

Trying to fish a piece of fruit from her large tropical drink, Julie replies, "Because we have to drive a half hour to get home after drinking these killer drinks where you don't taste the alcohol or know that you're drunk until it's too late."

Anne raises her hand, as though she is a student in grammar school wanting to be called upon. And Julie points at her as if she is the teacher in the classroom. "Anne, do you have a question?"

"I volunteer to be the designated driver the next time we want to do this," Anne replies.

Paige raises her coconut shell drink. "I'll drink to that."

We are bombed out of our minds. We had been partying for hours with very little food in their stomachs.

By late evening, it appears that Laurel is feeling the effects of the alcohol. She grips the edge of the table as she tries to stand up.

"I have to go to the restroom," she says.

I glance at the long line for the ladies' room. "I'll go with you."

We wander over to the back of the line and wait.

Laurel moans, "This line isn't moving."

"It is," I assure her. "It's just moving very slowly."

As Laurel and I near the entrance to the restroom, a woman walks out and announces, "Only one toilet is working."

The line of women groan, and complain so loudly that it attracts the attention of half the bar.

Laurel finally makes it inside the door to the restroom while I wait outside and pass the time by looking at a wall containing pictures of happy drunken patrons who had previously visited the touristy establishment.

I blink and look closer at what must be an alcohol induced figment of my imagination. I look away and back again. There behind the glass is a photo of Matt and Rosa in a romantic embrace.

I feel that inner hurricane from months earlier forming in the pit of my stomach. I'm overtaken by a swirling mass of dark clouds. I'm dizzy and feel like I'm going to vomit. I place my hand on the wall for support. I blink a few times and look again, hoping my eyes are playing tricks on me in my current state of inebriation.

I hear someone say, "It's your turn."

A woman touches my shoulder. "Hey, are you alright?"

I can't speak. Every pair of eyes in the line is on me. Panic stricken, I move out of line. Light headed, I look for Laurel. She's still in the restroom. I look around the bar and finally spot Paige. She sees that something is wrong.

Paige rushes to my side. "Are you sick? What's the matter?"

I point at the picture. Paige's eyes shoot wide open. "Holy Shit."

Laurel staggers out of the restroom and sees the photograph we're looking at. "Oh my God. Is this the flight attendant?"

"No," Paige says. "It's the girlfriend of the drug dealer we sent to prison."

With a purposefully sober gait, Paige walks over to the bartender and tells him something. Within minutes, the club manager comes over to the photo gallery. Paige displays her badge and points. "We need that picture."

"Talk about a buzz kill," Karen says as we sober up over coffee at a sidewalk café. "Did you ever suspect that Matt was seeing that woman?"

"She's very pretty," Laurel says, hiccupping as she looks at the photograph.

"And very dead," Paige replies.

"I was removed from the investigation before I discovered that Matt was cheating," I reply. "It never occurred to me that Londono would try to blackmail me or Matt with something like this."

"Maybe this wasn't about blackmail," Paige says. "What if Londono or Rosa had Matt bringing drugs into the country on his flights?"

I point a drunken finger at Paige. "The fire was not about Matt getting my money or assets." I shrug. "Alright, maybe a little. The night of the fire, I tried to scare him into admitting he had a girlfriend, so I told him we were going to review months of our phone records and determine which towers the calls were pinging off of. I'll bet he didn't want me or us to find out about his relationship with Rosa. I don't think he knew she was linked to my case until I told him about her death."

"The calls we thought one of Londono's men made from a location near Rosa's house must have been Rosa calling Matt," Paige adds.

With my elbows on the table top, I rest my forehead in my hands. "He freaked out that day at the airport when I said her name. When I questioned him about it, he said he knew a flight attendant by that name, and thought it was her. Damn, so many things I should have looked into, rather than taking his word for it."

"He could have been taking drug proceeds to banks off shore," Julie offers.

I shrug. "You're right. He had a lot of flights to the Bahamas, and up until recently, flight crews were not required to go through TSA screening. We need to meet with Mullaney immediately."

CHAPTER 31

Despite it being a Saturday afternoon, Mullaney agrees to meet with me and Paige at the U.S. Attorney's Office. We review all the documents from Londono's trial, only this time looking at them with Matt in mind.

Mullaney treats my allegations against Matt as accusations of a disgruntled ex-wife until Steve arrives with customs records documenting trips taken by Rosa to the Bahamas on Matt's airline.

"This new information should make you feel better," Steve says to me. "You thought Londono was coming after you and he was, just not in the way you thought. It was no coincidence that Rosa was flying on Matt's airline."

"Without the Bahamian bank records, we can't prove anything," Mullaney says. "This is all circumstantial evidence. All I can do is set up a meeting with Londono and his attorney to see if Londono wants to shave a few years off his sentence by telling us how Matt was involved."

"After attending Londono's sentencing, I thought it was finally over," Steve says. "But once again here I sit with you three, still trying to figure out how far-reaching Londono's tentacles really are."

***

Tuesday morning, Paige, Steve, and I meet Mullaney in his office. "What did Londono say about the photograph of Matt with Rosa?" I ask.

"I met with Mr. Londono and his attorney yesterday," Mullaney says. "Mr. Londono claims that he didn't know anything about Rosa ever meeting Matt and Mr. Londono's attorney suggested that Rosa did that on her own."

"That's bullshit." Paige says. "We all know that Matt was played by Rosa, at Londono's instruction. She would never have sought him out on her own."

"I agree," I say with a lash of anger. "Londono learned that Matt was a pilot and had Rosa see if she could get Matt to do something illegal."

"I'm no financial investigator," Steve says, "But we need to see if Londono has a bank account in the Bahamas. Maybe there's more to this than getting pictures of Matt with Rosa. Maybe Londono had his girlfriend depositing cash into an account over there."

"I don't think we'll get anything," Mullaney replies. "Most of those banks cater to criminals. Pay-offs and bribes are an everyday occurrence in the Bahamas. By now Londono would have paid someone to destroy any records that may have existed." Mullaney glances at the photo of Matt and Rosa. "Sorry, but Matt and his attorney also deny any wrongdoing."

"What?" I sit up in my chair. "Matt has an attorney?"

"Yes," Mullaney replies. "Most people call a criminal attorney when federal agents show up on their doorstep with questions." Mullaney stands and slips his arms into his black suit jacket. "I called in a favor and had Atlanta DEA pay Matt a visit. His lawyer claims that Matt was out with his friends and got drunk. That some woman flirted with Matt, and the photograph was taken of the two of them. End of story." Mullaney shrugs. "Londono could have planned to set Matt up so he could use the photo against him, but according to Matt, there was no blackmail attempt. I dug a little further and reviewed the evidence logs documenting everything we collected at Rosa's house, Londono's house, and the other search warrant sites. No such photo was ever discovered."

"No," I counter. "What makes more sense is that Rosa threatened to send me the photo if Matt didn't help her

smuggle money out of the country or smuggle drugs into the
United States."

Mullaney starts to speak, but I hold my hand up.
"There are two reasons why I think Matt was taking drug
money offshore. First and foremost, Steve and I found the
dates when Rosa was on Matt's flights. I wanted to go to the
Bahamas with Matt on a few of those flights, but he steered
me away from doing that. Secondly, and most damning of all,
is the fact that I found a lot of unexplained cash that Matt had
hidden at our house. That must have been payment for
helping Rosa."

Mullaney stares out his window, which offers a grand
view of Broward County. "I'm sorry, Jennifer. We have a lot
of circumstantial evidence connecting Matt with Rosa, but we
don't have enough to charge him. Maybe if Rosa had
mentioned him in that letter she wrote, but she didn't."

Steve interjects, "We pulled the passenger and crew
manifest for trips she made to the Bahamas. Matt was the
captain on some of Rosa's flights."

I hear myself say, "Matt probably set that up."

Even though I told myself that I was looking for
justice, deep down, I probably did want revenge.

"Can we prove that Matt booked her flight, or for that
matter, even knew she was on the flight?" Mullaney shakes
his head and smirks. "Come on. You folks know this. It's not
a crime to fly to the Bahamas. It's also not a crime for Matt to
get involved with a drug dealer's girlfriend. It's stupid, but
not a crime. To make a case against him, we need to prove
that he knew she was smuggling and that he conspired with
her to facilitate the movement of funds or drugs." Mullaney
turns away from the window and glares at us. "Can you do
that?"

We say nothing.

"I didn't think so," he replies. "DEA Atlanta
conducted interviews with Matt's co-pilots and various
airline personnel. There is nothing to implicate Matt in any

illegal activity. I have no doubt that Matt was played, either knowingly or unknowingly. Until we have proof of guilt, Matt is presumed innocent." Mullaney glances at his watch. "I have a meeting in five minutes. I'm sorry, but this is one of those rare cases that takes its toll on everyone." His eyes meet mine. "Some of us more than others."

CHAPTER 32

Seated in a four by four room that one could easily become claustrophobic in if it were not for the large thick glass window in the top portion of the door, I wait for Londono and reflect on the three years I had played cat and mouse with him.

The man who appears before me is much thinner than the one I had arrested months earlier. Londono shuffles into the room wearing an orange jumpsuit. He is bound in handcuffs and ankle cuffs. A smirk crosses his face when he sees me. Never taking his eyes off me, he takes a seat in the empty chair across the table.

"Tap on the glass when you're finished," the guard says before leaving and closing the door.

I watch the tall, muscular officer join two other guards behind a large workstation, facing our interview room.

Londono seems mildly amused. "Is my attorney meeting with us?"

"No, I wanted to meet with you alone."

He looks out at the guards who are busy processing a middle-aged white male that FBI agents had just brought in. "What do you think I know?"

I wait for him to make eye contact with me before I answer. "This should never have gotten personal. You were conducting business and I was doing my job."

Londono stares into my eyes.

"I didn't go after your wife. I didn't involve your children, but for some reason you felt the need to bring my husband into the mix."

He leans forward and coldly asks, "What do you want? Do you want me to tell you he was doing business with me so you can arrest him and make him pay for all the pain he has caused you?"

"No," I casually reply. "I divorced him. I haven't seen him in months. He's dead to me. I just want closure. Can you understand that? This has nothing to do with the Appeal your attorney has filed. I don't need you to admit to anything or implicate yourself. This conversation doesn't even leave this room unless you want to tell me something that can be used against Matt. My understanding is that AUSA Mullaney has already asked you and your attorney those questions and you had nothing to offer."

I pause and lean forward. "What I'm asking you for is some answers for me personally."

Staring into Londono's cold dark eyes, I say, "I'm a lot like you in that I want to know who I can trust, who is loyal to me."

Londono watches me, assessing my sincerity, but says nothing.

As a last ditch effort to get some answers from him, I say, "I'm leaving the task force. Actually, I'm leaving South Florida. This has changed both of our lives drastically. All I'm asking for is a hypothetical story, a theory about my husband's involvement."

He once again glances out at the guards, which says to me, the conversation is over. He's not going to talk. It was a long shot. Before visiting the prison, I doubted that he would tell me anything I didn't already know, but I had to try.

I push my chair back from the table and start to stand.

Londono taps on the table with his knuckles and motions for me to sit back down. "In my business, it is often useful to have leverage over your adversary," he says. "It is easy to manipulate a married man who has an eye for beautiful young women. These men are vulnerable and don't realize when they are being used." Londono leans back in his chair. "But sometimes young women, like Rosa, fall in love and when they do, they can become ruthlessly cunning, all in an attempt to get what they want." Londono shrugs. "Maybe the young woman tries to find a way to have the wife of the man she has fallen in love with removed from the picture." He leans forward. "She may also be foolish enough to betray those she is close to."

I couldn't believe that Londono was sharing this information. But what did he have to lose.

I tried to remain expressionless. Did Londono set the whole thing in motion because he thought Matt's involvement would destroy the government's case, only to have his plan fail because Rosa betrayed him?

I think back to the phone call where Rosa asked Londono to kill me. I didn't know Rosa but, probably per Londono's instructions, she had sought Matt out and seduced him.

Rosa wanted it all, Matt and millions of dollars from the sale of the cocaine that she was holding for Londono. That is why she told Londono that Steve and I took the cocaine. She was hoping that Londono or the Colombians would kill me, and that Londono would be charged with the murder. That would solve everything for her.

Londono leans back in his chair and smiles. "I shower women with gifts in exchange for their loyalty. But, I also know that you have to keep an eye on beautiful women like Rosa."

We sit in silence for a minute, staring at each other. Londono stands.

I motion for the guard to take Londono back to his cell where he will remain locked behind gray, dreary prison walls for many years.

Seated in the small bleak room alone, still processing the conversation, I realize that everything I had heard about Londono was true. He is very intelligent and not the type to leave anything to chance. He had his people watching Rosa. Londono knew what she was up to, and based on Theo Rojas' testimony, her untimely demise was per Londono's orders. It was never about the missing cocaine. Londono probably has money buried in thirty-gallon metal drums all around South Florida. Londono spoke with me because he wanted me to know that he was nobody's fool.

***

Seated at my desk in my home office, I smirk and toss the last of our household's personal receipts into a folder. If only Rosa knew how little she meant to Matt.

The phone records and credit card statements showed that he was again running around with the chubby flight attendant within days of Rosa's death. Matt was a Don Juan who would seduce women and move on to the next as the opportunity presented itself. I toss the folder into a drawer.

Maybe Rosa and I were not so different. I wanted Matt and a career. Rosa wanted Matt and the money. Both of us reaching, reaching, and almost grabbing the brass ring, only to have it plucked from our grasp.

I meander out to the patio. The night air is warm, and the scent of gardenia wafts in the breeze. I dip my toes in the pool and wonder, would Rosa have ever told Matt about her association with Londono? Doubtful, she would run the risk of losing him.

The more I think about it, the more I believe that Matt would never agree to be involved in their criminal activity, and run the risk of losing the career he loved and worked so hard for. He was just Londono's pawn and Rosa's way out.

Rosa must have manipulated Matt, just as she had done with so many other men. The money Matt had hidden away was probably payment for favors he had done for her involving violations of airline regulations, but not federal laws.

Matt was a liar, a cheat, and a charming opportunist, but not a drug trafficker or money launderer. Rosa probably told Matt that she had family in the Bahamas and needed to get a television over to them. Working for an airline that transported passengers and cargo, Matt could have transported merchandise to the Bahamas for her, not knowing that thousands of dollars were concealed in the goods he delivered.

In the end, it's just speculation. All that really matters to me is that it's finally over. Matt and Londono are out of my life permanently.

I stroll back into my home office and sit down at the computer. I pull up the title page of the book I have begun writing, *How to Keep Other Women Away from your Husband's Cockpit.*

I smirk and tap on the keyboard. Maybe something good will eventually come from this after all.

THE END

Made in the USA
Coppell, TX
29 October 2021

64855576R00108